The Secret of

Book 1 in the Hist

MW01103794

To Julie who always believed in me and my writing.
And Beth, the best sister a person could have.

www.FuzzyPawProductions.com is production liaison for
www.historymysteryforkidz.com
Cover design by FuzzyPawProductions.com
Graphics used with permission of Darren Hester
Photographers model: Haley Coe

ISBN   798-1-60458-476-9

1. Historical fiction—Juvenile fiction.
2. Civil War—Juvenile fiction

Published in the USA by www.instantpublishing.com

The Secret of Ghost Island

By Ellen Harveaux

Table of Contents

1. Quaker Clothes.................................9

2. The Runaway.................................23

3. Art Day at School.................................40

4. The Trip North.................................50

5. The Bounty Hunters.................................57

6. The New Baby.................................63

7. Rumors.................................78

8. Art Class.................................89

9. Trip to the General Store.................................99

10. Papa's Return.................................113

11. The Answer.................................127

12. Exploring the Island.................................131

13. Waiting.................................136

14. More Waiting.................................152

15. Hurry and Hide.................................175

The Secret of Ghost Island

Quaker Clothes

" Be quiet, Old Biddy," eleven-year-old
Hannah Haviland said. "I'm trying to gather thy eggs,
not wring thy neck for Sunday dinner." The hen
flapped and fussed, tossing grain, straw and feathers
all over Hannah's somber black dress. Hannah
sighed. She hated her black Quaker clothes. There
was only one other older Quaker student who
attended with her at the schoolhouse, a boy and not
a target for the teasing as she was.

Hannah hid her frustration with her clothes from her parents. At school, she was the only girl dressed in black garb from the tip of her leather boots to her coal shuttle-shaped bonnet that hid her face and hair from everyone. It wouldn't be so bad if she weren't an artist who loved the colors in God's creation. And now that it was spring and the Ohio flowers were coming into bloom and the trees were starting to sprout leaves, she felt her disgust even more.

Girls at school, with their colorful dresses with little sprigs of flowers, and their braids tied with multi-colored ribbons made her feel her difference even more. Their hair was allowed to be long and free while all of hers was trapped under an ugly cap.

She knew that the other girls giggled and poked fun behind her back at her required clothes, but she pretended not to care, staying to herself during lunch and walking to and from school alone.

10

After double-checking the lock on the chicken coop, Hannah scurried across the farmyard toward the porch. She needed to get the eggs to her mother who was preparing breakfast and then take the breakfast meal down to her father and brother at Black Oak Meadow.

A huge Oak tree that stood on the corner of the cornfield had at one time been struck by lightening which hollowed out the insides and left the bark blackened on one side, the side that faced away from the meadow. From that view, the tree looked normal. The side facing toward the soon-to-be cornfield was green and healthy. The destroyed half of the tree was like a small charred room, hidden with new growth. Hannah was amazed that enough of the tree had survived the bolt of fire to keep on living. When she was younger, she and her bother, Aaron, had played hide and seek in the little room-sized hole.

Her father and brother had been up since before dawn to finish the plowing. Corn had to be planted soon, and during planting time it was her job to gather the eggs, sweep the porch and then ride her pony Princess down to the field to take breakfast sandwiches to the men that were plowing. The men didn't want to stop to come back to the house to eat. She then had to rush to get to school before the last bell rang.

At noon, her brother would come back to the house to fetch lunch. Mrs. Haviland, had in the past taken the meals down to the fields, but this year she was ready to have a baby and Hannah's father didn't want her making the half-mile trek in her condition.

The ground had finally thawed, as had the river and, as Pa said, "springtime was for planting corn and moving the slaves on the Underground Railroad."

When she entered the kitchen, her mother was slicing bacon and laying it strip by strip into the cast iron skillet where it sizzled and sputtered. Nothing smelled better to her than the scent of bacon cooking. She sniffed appreciatively as she set the egg basket near the kitchen pump and began washing the eggs. When she finished, her mother turned from her cooking to give her instructions.

"Hannah, thee needs to slice the bread for the bacon and egg sandwiches I'm making. But first run down to the cellar and get a fresh jar of my raspberry preserves for the jelly bread. Thee will need to hurry so not be late for school again!" Mrs. Haviland raised her eyebrow meaningfully as she caught Hannah's eye. "Thee has been daydreaming again."

Hannah protested. "Only just a little this morning."

Her mother gave her a look. "A little is too much when we have such busy mornings. Hurry now."

At the top of the stairs, Hannah hitched up her skirts and fairly skimmed the top of the steps as she ran down into the cellar, where all the jars of canning were kept neatly on the shelves. She made the trip down and back in just a few minutes.

She scrambled to slice bread for the breakfast sandwiches and for the jelly bread, which was rather like a dessert treat for the middle of the morning to tide the men over until the noon lunch. Once the sandwiches and the jelly bread were packed into the wicker hamper, Mrs. Haviland started pumping water into an oaken bucket for Hannah to carry.

Both the hamper and the bucket had rope handles that hooked easily over the saddle horn.

Hannah ran to get Princess, saddled. She pulled the Paint mare up next to the porch while her mother hooked the breakfast things onto Hannah's saddle. "Ride carefully, dear," her mother admonished, patting Hannah's shoulder with affection. "Go slow."

Hannah rode cautiously down the beaten path. When she got there, she found that her father and brother had plowed half the field already. Even though the morning held the light chill of April, Hannah saw that they were sweating freely, their coats off and hanging on the fence. Their sleeves were rolled up above their elbows.

Aaron saw her first and whistled for his plow horse to stop. He was quickly beside Princess, relieving Hannah of the hamper and the bucket of water. He was tall and thin like her father. He had the dark hair and eyes that matched Hannah's

"Pa. Food." He hollered as he gave Hannah's nose an affectionate tweak. "Thank thee, freckle face for bringing us food. I am so hungry, I'm ready to eat the whole side of a cow."

Hannah giggled as she slid from the saddle. She took off Princess's saddle and tied the mare to a fence post to eat grass. Aaron would need the horse to go fetch lunch and more water. She gave a wave to her dad who was walking slowly across the plowed field and ran back down the path she had just traveled. She still had to eat her own breakfast, pack her lunch pail and head on to school.

In the kitchen, her mother had left some sandwiches on the table for Hannah to eat. Finished with making breakfast, Mrs. Haviland was now kneading bread dough. Hannah glanced silently at her mother and whispered a blessing of thanks to God for the food. Along with her prayer she sent up a request for the new, soon-to-be-born baby and asked that the birthing would be easy for her mother. Since Hannah was born, her mother had already lost three babies in childbirth. Hannah wanted this one to live. And she prayed secretly that the baby would be a boy. It was too depressing to be a Quaker girl.

As she walked along the road, slowly, she did pay attention to the school bell clanging in the distance but the sound didn't make her hurry any faster. She was noticing instead, the many shades of green in the world and her fingers itched to copy those colors onto a piece of art paper. The featherings of gray, white and brown fur in the squirrel overhead, who was chattering angrily as she passed under his branch, captured her interest so that she didn't even notice that the second bell was now ringing.

A blue jay screeched by her bonnet, guarding her nest, Hannah assumed. Something inside her head was shouting at her to capture these rich images. She wanted to shout to someone, anyone, that God's creation was full of varied hues, not just black and white.

Finally when she realized that the third and last bell was ringing, she shook herself out of her daydreams and began running toward the school house, trying to remember how long she had been dawdling and bracing herself for another lunch time detention.

Just as she expected, for being late again, Hannah had to stay in for lunch recess to clean the blackboards and beat the erasers. It didn't matter to her, though. She often ate by herself and took walks along the creek alone. Most of the other girls had their own interests that didn't include Hannah.

That afternoon when she got home, her mother was stitching on some baby clothes. Beside her rocking chair, her mother kept a mending basket, always full of clothes and socks that needed attention. The basket always seemed to stay full no matter how many things her mother repaired.

Hannah kissed her mother's cheek and lay her books and her bonnet down on the table next to the rocker. "Hannah, dear," her mother said, "get thee something to eat before thee does thy chores." She looked closely at Hannah. "Thee looks tired today. Is thee sick?" She pulled Hannah's face towards hers and felt for a sign of fever. Hannah shook her head no and after giving her mother another hug, went off to the kitchen to eat.

She smelled the savory stew bubbling quietly on the stove as she sliced some bread and slathered it with jelly. She could smell the cinnamon and sugar from the apple pie baking in the oven.

The huge grandfather clock ticking in the corner of the parlor chimed out four times by the time Hannah had changed into a work dress. She still had to milk the cows, put fresh straw in the horse stalls and take supper out to the fields.

She was just putting the second bucket of milk into the springhouse, to keep it chilled, when she heard a rustling in the bushes behind the pump. She glanced up to see what was making such a noise, thinking that it sounded much like an animal scuffling or fighting. She shivered, hoping that it wasn't an angry raccoon or another scary animal. She sloshed some milk over the side of the pail and onto her shoes. She made herself slow down and was careful to put the stone plate over the bucket to protect the milk and help chill it.

20

She had better pay attention to her job, she said to herself as she directed her eyes back to the springhouse. It was a small room dug into the side of a hill that had an underground spring running out of it. Her father had built a hard-packed dirt cave around the spring, put in a solid door and routed the spring to run across a stone floor before it ran under the walls and continued on its way into the woods. The combination of the stone, the cold water and the thick door kept the milk, butter, cheese and meat chilled even on the hottest day.

She was just putting the branch through the leather catch on the door, to keep the door locked against animals, when she heard the rustling again. But this time she heard more. More like a low growling sound.

The hairs stood up on the back of her neck, as she remembered the rabid dog her father had shot because he was wild and vicious. She took two steps back—away from the springhouse---she was trying to decide if she should run.   She kept her eyes glued on the rustling leaves as she continued to take one step at a time backwards.

Suddenly she saw two dark eyes peering out at her from the nearby bush, and then she saw a dark face covered with blood. As she watched, horror stricken, a black man in tattered clothes burst from the bushes and collapsed at Hannah's feet.

She wanted to scream, but it was stuck somewhere in her throat. Instead, she ran.

The Runaway

"Pa. Pa." Hannah ran as if a mad mother bear was nipping at her heels. She did not daydream along the path this time as she flew to the field to fetch her father.

Somewhere in her frightened mind, Hannah knew that the bleeding man that had fallen through the bushes was a runaway slave looking for shelter, and meant her no harm. Hannah had overheard the men at the Sunday Meeting House talking about helping slaves escape from their masters. Hannah was proud that the Quakers had a hand in helping slaves find a new home.

Hannah's town of Ripley, Ohio, people said, was the perfect place to aid those searching for freedom on the Underground Railroad. The

Underground Railroad was a series of homes that hid escaped slaves and helped them to travel to the next "station" or house that was willing to help them. Almost everyone at Hannah's church helped slaves escape north to Canada. Many of the church families had stations for the Underground Railroad in their homes.

Ohio was a "free" state and Kentucky, right across the Ohio River, was a "slave" state. Slaves often crossed the river at that point to gain their freedom. The river that separated those two states, near Ripley, was only 1,000 feet across at that location. Many runaway slaves from Kentucky followed the Maysville Road to the river and across it to liberty.

But children were not included in helping the runaways. When Friend Olsen had seen Hannah drinking in the men's conversation like someone

24

dying of thirst, he had shooed her away to play with the little children. She wished she had heard more, but she understood. A careless word, in the wrong place, could endanger the whole family and the slave.

Her breath was hitching in her lungs as she dashed across the freshly plowed field to reach her father on the other side.

"Pa. Pa" she yelled. Her father looked up from his team with alarm.

Twilight was creeping up on the spring day, starting to turn shadows into long fingers that reach darkly out over the dirt rows. She gulped as she tried to get her breath. Her father and brother had already begun running toward her. Fear sparked in her father's eyes.

"What is it, child?" he   demanded as he and Hannah met in the middle of the field. He put a calming hand on her shoulder as she tried to get her breath. "Is it the babe?"

"No, father," Hannah gulped, hiccupping over her words. "I think it's a slave. Thee must come quickly. I think he's dead."

Her father, tall, lanky and strong, looking much like the newly elected President Lincoln, picked her up easily as he started jogging toward Princess. Over his shoulder he hollered to her brother Aaron to bring the teams of horses back to the barn.

As they jogged, he swung her onto his back as if she were a feather pillow. "Hang on, Hannah," he said as he began running back to the house. She clung on and bumped along with him. "Why does thee think the slave is dead?" Hannah didn't even have to think about her answer. "All the blood, father.

26

I think he's very hurt." She went on to explain the rustling of the leaves and her fright as the man fell out of the bushes.

When they approached the springhouse, she was relieved to hear the slave moaning.

"Thank, God." Mr. Haviland said earnestly as he knelt down to carefully check the fallen black man.

He sat Hannah down gently then turned his attention to the injured man. "Run tell thy mother. Have her fix a bed in the root cellar for him. Then when Aaron gets here, have him come to help me carry this man into the house." Hannah turned to run when her father's large hand stopped her. He asked for her apron and after she stripped it off, he strode to the pump and wet it and rolled it into a ball. "I will try to wash off some of the blood before thy mother sees him."

Hannah ran to the house and was just mounting the steps when her brother, leading all the horses entered the barn. Hannah shouted to him, giving him their father's message and then went into the house to find her mother.

Mrs. Haviland went down into the cellar with Hannah and they made a soft pallet on the floor behind shelves filled with jars of preserves.

Aaron and Mr. Haviland brought the man slowly down the steps. They arranged him on the cot and began stripping off his dirty shirt to put on a clean one belonging to Mr. Haviland. "If he's this battered, "her father said, "I'm sure the bounty hunters will be close behind. We must take care."

The slave roused long enough to explain his name was Elijah. When he saw the black Quaker clothing on the family, he heaved a sigh of relief. He knew that he was in safe hands. He just had a chance to murmur his thanks when he fell asleep.

Mrs. Haviland layered several quilts over the large black man. "He is going hot and cold, Daniel. I fear that he is going to develop a fever. I'm worried."

Hannah saw that her mother's dark brown eyes were troubled with anxiety and a frown creased her forehead. Aaron had not uttered a word since Hannah had dashed to the field earlier. Everyone seemed to be in a state of shock. Three pairs of eyes looked to Mr. Haviland for answers.

"I will ask Friend Olsen what to do. He has experience with these things. I will ride over there after supper. Everything must seem normal in case someone is watching our house. We must act as if nothing has changed."

But Hannah knew that everything had changed. Slave hunters had the government's permission to bring a slave back from wherever they had run. Even to a free state. Having their houses and barns burned could punish those who harbored slaves. Not everyone in Ohio was sympathetic to the plight of the runaways.

That evening Hannah hurried through her homework to spend time watching Elijah down in the root cellar. While she was there, his sleep was restless and he mumbled things over and over. Hannah couldn't understand what he was saying.

About nine, Aaron came down to take his turn. He asked Hannah how Elijah was doing. "He's very restless. And hot. I think his fever is getting worse. He keeps throwing off his blankets and talking nonsense. I'm not sure but I think he's getting worse."

Her brother, three years older, and at fourteen considered a man, looked troubled too. "Thee is right, Hannah. He looks worse. Pa isn't back from the Olsen's yet. I wonder what the oversight committee will decide to do with Elijah?"

Since their move to Ohio a year ago, the Havilands hadn't really been involved personally in the Underground Railroad as yet. Hannah knew that the oversight committee at the Meeting House had more knowledge of how to take care of the runaways and avoid the bounty hunters.

The next day at noon, sitting on a small stonewall that surrounded the meadow by the school, Hannah felt herself worrying about the slave, so worried in fact that she couldn't eat her lunch. Her imagination was filled with all kinds of thoughts of bounty hunters and running slaves. She barely touched her biscuits thick with ham and mustard. She finally sat that aside and took some dainty bites of her mother's apple pie. No matter how upset she was, she could never pass up a piece of her mother's pie. A shadow fell across her and she started in fear, jerked out of her daydreaming.

She sighed in relief when she saw it was just Jonathan Olsen, son of the man who had warned her about listening to the adult's conversation. His white blond hair was so fine that it usually hung in his eyes and he was always pushing it under his hat where it only stayed for a minute. He had the twinkling blue eyes of his mother.

He was the only other Quaker child in school near her age. He was thirteen and would be graduating at the end of May. Most of the other Quaker children in schools were little first or second graders.

He gave Hannah a knowing look before he sat beside her on the wall. His flat brimmed black hat looked as odd as her black bonnet among all the bareheaded students playing in the meadow. Seeing him brought back her shame of feeling different.

"Thy father came to our house last night. Thee has a surprise visitor." It wasn't a question.

Hannah raised shocked eyes to Jonathan. "Thee knows that we are not supposed to talk about those things. Thy father was very angry when I listened to the men talking at the Meeting House."

Jonathan smiled. Not much disturbed Jonathan. He didn't even seem to resent his drab clothes. "I know but it was a lively discussion at our house last night. The elders are trying to decide what to do. Evidently there have been several runaways crossing the river since the ice melted and many are hiding slaves. My father said the slave would probably have to stay at thy house for a while until they can move the others. "

"He's very sick and my mother is worried." She continued telling him the story of her finding him and his feverish condition. The bell rang signaling the end of lunchtime.

By the time the family sat down to dinner that evening, Daniel Haviland began explaining about the conference at the Olsen's house. It was similar to what Jonathan had said.

Over the mashed potatoes and fried chicken, Daniel explained that no one more experienced in the workings of the Underground Railroad could take the slave off their hands. And if the slave's injuries got worse, the Havilands would have to transport the slave on their own to a Quaker doctor further north.

"But I am concerned for thee, Rachel." Daniel said to his wife sitting at the other end of the table. "Thee does not need the extra work of caring for one more person, especially someone so ill. I worry about thy health and the coming baby. Thy strength…" His words stopped as he looked at his wife with loving eyes.

What he didn't say, Hannah knew, was his worry about the babies she had already lost. He didn't want that to happen again. Hannah remembered it had been so much sorrow for her mother.

But tonight her mother seemed strong. "Thee must not worry, Daniel. I believe that it was God's hand that brought Elijah to us. We must care for him. We may not know as much as the other families, but we can learn."

That evening when Hannah was finished washing the dishes, she took her turn down in the cellar keeping watch over the moaning Elijah. He was half asleep and half awake. When he seemed to be awake, she tried to get him to sip a spoonful of warm chicken broth. After taking several sips, he seemed to rouse and his eyes focused on her. He grabbed her by the wrist and pulled her closer as if to tell her a secret.

"Where's my babies?" He asked, looking around the root cellar with confusion. "My babies supposed to be coming soon. To meet me. They's coming. They promised they was a coming."

Hannah wasn't sure what he was talking about. She tried to reassure him. He was looking frightened. "I'm sure they're coming Friend Elijah," she said.

The big man seemed reassured and lay back down, falling back into a restless sleep.

36

That night, when Mrs. Haviland was tucking Hannah in bed and hearing her prayers, Hannah told her mother about the strange comment Elijah had made.

"He said his babies were coming Mama. Does thee think that his children are coming too?"

"I don't know Hannah. It's hard to be sure since he's been so feverish. A lot of what he says doesn't make sense. " After her mother left, Hannah would not give up the idea that Elijah's children were coming to find him. Her sleep that night was filled with troublesome dreams of Elijah's children looking for him and not being able to find him.

Hannah woke with dark smudges under her eyes, showing just how restless her sleep had been. Her mother gave her a sharp look at breakfast, but said nothing.

Later, at school, her eyes felt scratchy and she felt like she could fall asleep any minute. Every time she thought of her dream, she sent up a quick prayer for the safety of Elijah's children, if they were trying to find their father.

That night, again, Elijah woke up and told Hannah that he was sure his two little girls were running away to meet up with him. He was supposed to have met them at the river, but he missed them. He was sure they were still on the way.

"My babies are named Goodness and Mercy, " he said. "Just like the Bible. Goodness and Mercy will follow me all the days of my life."

"How old are they?" Hannah asked. Elijah peered at her closely. "They's about your age, Miss. They be my twin daughters. Born ten years ago but they was sold last year to another plantation. I sent word to them where to meet me. I don't even know if they got the message." That was the longest conversation that Hannah had with Elijah and the talking seemed to tire him. He fell back into his troubled sleep calling out now and then for Goodness and Mercy to hurry.

Art Day at School

Friday! Friday was Hannah's favorite day at school since Miss Perkins, their teacher with the beautiful blonde hair and colorful dresses, taught the children art after second recess on Friday afternoons. On Art Day she brought in her collection of colored pencils, watercolors, pastel chalk and oil paints. She also supplied art paper. Hannah suspected that Miss Perkins was from a rich family back east who sent her art supplies whenever she asked for them.

The first time Miss Perkins had introduced the new subject there was muttering and groaning from the boys, who would rather go outside and have running contests in the meadow than sit still for art lessons. However, as the weeks had gone on, the boys eventually began enjoying themselves.

40

The girls had always been more agreeable, oohing and aahing over the variety of choices.

Usually Miss Perkins would let the students draw what they wanted but she always had something they could copy if they wished. In the fall they drew colored leaves, pumpkins and fall trees. During the winter she made an arrangement of pinecones, branches with lichen designs, and sprays of holly and ivy.

Christmas brought pictures of the Nativity scene complete with wise men and shepherds. Easter was paintings of the Resurrection and the empty tomb. Miss Perkins brought in some paintings by those people she called "The Old Masters."

The boys, after a bout of grumbling and complaining, began to enjoy the art lessons too, as Miss Perkins encouraged each and every one to experiment with their own ideas, styles and choices of medium.

This Friday, when the students came clattering back into the classroom after lunch, Miss Perkins had arranged some bright yellow daffodils in a large crystal vase. Hannah's hand was itching to sketch them. After her sketch was finished, she planned to do the painstaking watercolor washes that would bring them to life on paper.

She noticed on her way up to the front to get some paper and pencils, that Jonathan's head was bent in concentration over a charcoal sketch of a squirrel running up the side of a tree. It was surprisingly good. His fingers were smudged and there were streaks of black on his white shirt. She was impressed how cleverly he had captured the mischievous nature of the animal. She couldn't help herself, she had to stop and stare. Jonathan was a good artist and she said so.

"Thee are a clever artist, Jonathan. I can almost hear him chatter."

Jonathan smiled his thanks. "I think I'm good at drawing animals because of all the hunting I do."

Hannah thought about that a moment then shook her head. "No, thee are talented with art, not just hunting. I could not sketch something unless it was sitting in front of me. Thy art is in thy fingers and in thy memory."

Miss Perkins came up behind Hannah and laid a hand on her shoulder while she looked at Jonathan's sketch. "Good job, Jonathan."

She left them and walked around the room encouraging other students on their work in progress. One of the things that Hannah liked about Miss Perkins was that she always said something nice about each attempt. Even praising those whose attempts were less than artistic.

Before she got her paper, Hannah had to make one more comment to Jonathan. "Only one thing would make thy picture better, Jonathan." She smiled. "Color." With that she went back to her seat and began the task of drawing the daffodils.

The whole afternoon sped by as Hannah sketched and painted. Time disappeared as she bit her lip and tried her skill at making the daffodils appear under the tip of her pencil. Once she was satisfied with the sketch, she meticulously began applying the faint washes of yellow and green until she was satisfied with the finished product.

Miss Perkins appeared at her shoulder. "How beautiful, Hannah! You have captured the essence of the flowers." Hannah was pleased with the dreamy,

44

misty look of the flowers. Miss Perkins continued. "I think you have made your painting even more beautiful than the original flowers."

Hannah was shocked! Was her picture more beautiful than God's creation? Never! But she wisely kept her mouth shut and just said thanks.

"Your watercolor puts me in mind of the Impressionists, Hannah. If you lived in Europe, I'm sure you would belong to that school of art. However, they did not use watercolor but oils. You have achieved much the same effect as theirs. You should be proud of your accomplishment today."

All the way home, Hannah's feet hardly touched the ground, so pleased was she with her picture. She was so happy that she forgot the drab colors of her clothes for once. She skipped along the road and noticed all the vivid spring colors ---the red of new shoots, the startling blue of the sky, and the shy purple violets peeking out from under their dark green leaves, hiding at the base of the oaks.

Mrs. Haviland was sitting on the front porch churning butter when Hannah got home. She wiped her hands on her apron, and gently took the picture Hannah had made, so she could look at it closely. Hannah didn't realize she was holding her breath until her mother looked up at her and smiled.

"Hannah, thee has such a talent. It is such a gift from God. I wasn't sure that art lessons at school were a good idea. But thy talent has proved me wrong. We must get thy father to make a frame for this. I want to hang it over the mantel so that during the long, cold winter nights, we'll still be able to see the promise of spring."

She gave Hannah a quick hug and reached to pin back her glowing red hair that was falling out of its severe bun. Hannah often wished she had been born

46

with the color of her mother's hair. All of Hannah's hair and eyes just blended in with her Quaker clothes---dark hair and dark eyes like her father and brother. She imagined that she looked like one of Jonathan's charcoal pictures, with no touch of color to be seen. Her mother had bright red, curly hair and green eyes, the color of the spring leaves. Why couldn't she have colorful looks?

Biddy was cranky again as Hannah gathered eggs that afternoon. Even though father had said that their schedules should stay unchanged since the arrival of Elijah. the slave, much had changed. Aaron and her father no longer plowed from twilight until dark, eating their meals down on the fields.

They now came to the house for all their meals; father explained that the men should stay close because of the baby's near arrival and the sickness of Elijah.

In her heart, Hannah also knew that the unstated reason for her father's closeness to the house was the real threat of the bounty hunters always on the prowl for runaways.

Elijah still wove in and out of comas and Mrs. Haviland was getting extremely anxious about his fever. It seemed to be getting worse. Last night Hannah's father had mentioned the need to take Elijah to a Quaker doctor further north.

Her dreams that night were laced with bounty hunters with flaming torches chasing two little black girls through the woods. She woke up trembling, hearing the old clock downstairs bonging out the message of four o'clock. She was afraid to go back to sleep and was still awake when the sky outside turned from pink to blue.

Sunday the family went to the Meeting House with all the other Quaker families. Hannah saw

Jonathan and his brothers after the service, as the adults gathered in one group to talk and the children in another group.

She saw her father talking worriedly with the elders of the church and she kept her distance. She knew they were coming up with a plan to take Elijah further north for medical help. She couldn't help remembering her dream of the two little slave girls running through the woods looking for their father. She prayed that they would find him. And soon.

The Trip North

That evening, Hannah held a metal basin of water while her mother gently wiped Elijah's forehead to cool his fever. He was still on the cot in the root cellar, but he had kicked off his blankets and his clothes were soaked through with sweat. Hannah' mother was clearly upset that Elijah seemed to be worse.

"Hannah," she said softly, turning away from the slave. "Father is taking Friend Elijah to the doctor tonight. I'm afraid that this dear man's wounds are getting worse, no matter what we do. He needs to get help tonight."

Hannah ran upstairs and out the back screen door, letting it bang shut loudly, something she was never supposed to do. If it hadn't been an emergency, she would have been scolded for the act.

It was twilight now, and as she ran into the barn she found her father and brother making ready the wagon to take Elijah north to the Quaker doctor. The two men piled the wagon with hay from the loft in the barn. Aaron was up in the loft, shoveling down hay while Mr. Haviland was in the wagon bed, arranging the hay so it would hide the slave. Her father had explained to the family over a quick, cold supper that the elders felt that he and Aaron should take the slave north as soon as it was dark. The other men in the Quaker families, there abouts, would help with the farming chores until the two men returned.

Mr. Haviland's only concern was for his wife and her condition. "Rachel," he said. "How can I leave thee? With the babe coming and all?" Hannah knew he was thinking about the other babies that didn't make it. "And I have to take Aaron so we can travel faster, up and back. One can drive while theother sleeps. Maybe someone else from the meeting can take Elijah?"

Hannah watched her mother's face change. She got what Mr. Haviland called, "her stubborn look." Mrs. Haviland's green eyes sparked with something close to anger. "Thee said it thyself, Daniel. There is no one else. Everyone has his or her own runaways to help. And Elijah has come to our door, not someone else's. The elders have no choice but to wait. We must help him now or he will die. I'm sure of it. I could not have that on my conscience. God has sent him to us and not others."

Hannah could see that her father had given in to her mother's persuasive speech.

"Aaron, ride to the Olsen's quickly and tell them the plan, then hurry back and help me ready the wagon. They will need to keep an eye on thy mother and sister." He turned to his wife as he rose from the dinner table. "Rachel, thee must prepare us food and water for the trip. Hannah, get me some fresh blankets from the linen closet. We'll wrap Elijah up warmly and hide him under a fresh load of hay. With darkness as our friend, and God's guidance for our trip, we'll make good time."

Each person scurried to do his or her appointed task. Hannah's thoughts, as she pulled quilts from the upstairs linen closet, were that not once were the bounty hunters mentioned. She shivered as she remembered her dream.

While others were preparing for the trip, Hannah was by Elijah's cot again, rubbing his head with a cool cloth. She touched his forehead. His skin was still hot and clammy. She prayed that they would be in time to save him.

Suddenly, Elijah lurched up to a sitting position. His eyes were wild and frenzied like the rabid dog her father had shot when he came into their yard, frothing at the mouth and slobbering.

Elijah grabbed Hannah's wrist. Elijah was trying to make her understand something. He pointed to the far wall. His voice was at once loud and soft.

"See! There they be. My girls. They's coming to follow me. Promise me that you will find them and save them. Watch for them!" he insisted. "Goodness and Mercy shall follow me all the days of my life. Promise me. Promise me, please!" He was gasping for breath now, squeezing Hannah's hand until it ached. "I will." She made the promise to him and to herself.

Elijah quieted down after that and soon her father and Aaron were wrapping his large body into blankets and hauling him up the stairs to the waiting wagon.

She and her mother stood on the back porch, lantern held aloft watching the two men ready everything for the trip. Elijah was hidden under the hay and the basket of food and the jugs of water were tucked under the bench seat of the wagon. Aaron was already on the seat, holding tight the reins of old Betsy and her daughter, Belle.

Daniel kissed his wife and ruffled Hannah's hair as he said good-bye. Worry was in his eyes. Mrs. Haviland put a finger to his lips as he was beginning to speak.

"Do not worry thyself, Daniel. I will be fine. The baby is lively and Mrs. Olsen will be close by if I need help. Nothing bad will happen while thee are gone. I promise thee.

"God will watch over us. If my time comes, Hannah can take the trap to fetch Mrs. Olsen. Hannah's no longer just a young child. She will pull her weight and be a great help to me. We will manage fine." She kissed her husband on the cheek and stood back to let him go. He turned and jogged down the steps and mounted the wagon seat.

"Thee take care. God be with thee."

As the wagon lumbered out of the yard and the circle of lamp light, Mrs. Haviland said quietly," God be with us all."

The Bounty Hunters

The banging on the front door roused Hannah from a deep sleep. From the darkness of the room she knew it wasn't yet dawn. She and her mother hadn't fallen asleep until after midnight, when the old clock was chiming twelve. Mrs. Haviland had insisted that she and Hannah must clean up the root cellar so that all traces of Elijah were erased.

Hannah crept down the stairs, hastily tying her wrapper around her nightgown. Her feet were cold on the wood floor of the hall. at the top of the stairs, that wound down to the front door. She looked over the banister to see what the commotion was. She heard her mother's voice raising, tinged with anger. Her father always teased that her mother had a redhead's temper and that it was wasted on a Quaker who always followed the path of peace.

Her mother wasn't peaceful right at the moment from the sound of it. She was raising her voice by degrees, arguing with someone on the front porch.

Hannah crept down further until she was looking around her mother's shoulder to peer at the mass of men on the front porch. They were rough and angry, stomping their boots and jingling their spurs, while her mother, very firmly refused them entrance into her home.

"I understand thy situation, sheriff," she said very firmly, "but I do not give thee permission to push by a woman large with child to search a house. Thee know that we do not hold with slavery, but I give thee my word as a Christian woman that there is no slave hiding in my house."

The sheriff looked perplexed. Behind him were bounty hunters straining to be able to find a slave and make money out of the deal, which conflicted with the sheriff's desire to act like a gentleman. He would have to live in this town long after the bounty hunters left. And he certainly didn't want to disturb a woman about to give birth. And she had given her word.

Hannah could see the doubt fighting in his eyes. A bounty hunter behind the sheriff made a rude comment about the Quakers, and that remark seemed to make the decision for the lawman. He turned and with gritted teeth, ordered the men off the porch.

Very sweetly, Mrs. Haviland said in her most honeyed voice, " Gentlemen, please feel free to search the grounds and the barn. And please take what water thee need for thy horses." She calmly shut the door and breathed a sigh of relief. "Hannah, dear." Please cut seven pieces of my apple pie and go out onto the back porch and offer it to the sheriff and the bounty hunters."

Hannah looked at her mother with confusion. Was she crazy to offer good apple pie to those...those...madmen out there? She could hear crashing and banging, as they looked everywhere.

Mrs. Haviland just patted her daughter's shoulder. "We need to appear unafraid and sure of ourselves. The apple pie will distract them for a while, hopefully. At least they didn't ask where thy father had gone so early in the morning."

Hannah dutifully cut the pie and put the slices on her mother's good china plates and carefully ferried the seven pieces out to the railing of the porch. Her mother was right. It did seem to calm their tempers and distract them from their frenzied searching.

Some of the men squatted in the yard to eat and others leaned against the porch railing to polish off the pie. Hannah stood quietly near the screen door and just watched the men. She wasn't used to seeing such men before. They seemed coiled like some poisonous snake, ready to strike.

Hannah collected the plates and forks when they were done and stacked the dirty dishes on an old table next to the door. She was just ready to go back inside, when one of the men approached her. He squatted down so that he was eye-level with her. "Where's your daddy so early this morning, little girl?" His eyes had a hard gleam.

Hannah hated it that she stuttered. "He had to take a load of hay into town." The bounty hunter stood up and put his empty plate on the table. "Mite early to be delivering hay, you ask me," he said to no one in particular. As the men filed out of the yard and found their horses, Hannah scurried back inside with the dishes. She knew her face was burning. She hoped that her answer wasn't truly a lie.

The New Baby

As she entered the kitchen, Hannah heard the men out in the yard complaining bitterly because they had found nothing. Her mother was sitting at the table.

"When those dreadful men leave, thee must hook up the buggy and go fetch Mrs. Olsen. The baby is on its way."

By the time Hannah changed her clothes, hitched the horse and reached the Olsen's farm, she could hear the school bell chiming in the distance, warning young scholars to hurry to school. There was ten minutes until the final bell. Hannah was unsure what to do next. Should she go to school or go back home to help Mrs. Olsen?

She tied the horse to a low hanging branch and ran up the steps to the Olsen's front door. Jonathan was coming around the corner of the house as she made to knock. He had his books wrapped with a leather strap, slung over his shoulder. In his other hand he had his metal lunch pail that had once been a molasses container. He looked at Hannah with a frown.

"Has thy mother started the birthing then?" When Hannah nodded, she turned and went down the steps again and met him at the bottom. She was just getting ready to explain what had happened with the bounty hunters, but before she had a chance, he bellowed for his mother.

When Mrs. Olsen appeared at the door, while wiping her hands with a dishtowel she motioned Hannah into the house. She had gray hair pulled into a bun. Her face was round like her body and her blue eyes were twinkling. She grabbed Hannah and gave her a swift hug and then released her to grab her hand to pull her down the hall into the kitchen at the back of the house.

"I've had to live all these years with seven sons and a husband. What a joy it would have been to have a beautiful daughter like thee around. All these noisy boys…I declare…" She released Hannah and laughed at the look on Jonathan's face. He seemed offended at his mother's comment. Hannah laughed at him too, enjoying the fact that someone thought girls were nice to have around.

"Thee needs to skip school for today, Jonathan. I need thee to stay at the Haviland's with me for a while. I need thee to haul water for me and be able to run home for thy father if those bounty hunters come annoying us at the Haviland's."

"They've already been to our house this morning." Hannah rushed to explain. "Before the sun came up they were pounding on the door. My mother wouldn't let them into the house. They were very angry, but they didn't come in."

"Good for her," said Mrs. Olsen said as she finished tidying the kitchen and reached for her bonnet. " Speak the truth in love, I say. They were here in the middle of the night and I refused them entrance too. I told them they should be ashamed of themselves for bothering God-fearing people in the middle of the night. It was downright rude if thee asks me."

"Jonathan. Saddle up thy horse and follow us. I'll go get my things." She turned to Hannah. "Thy father stopped by last night and told us about the situation. He asked us to watch out for thee. Jonathan can do some plowing today for thy family," and at his humorous groan, Mrs. Olsen patted him on the shoulder and said, "Thy brothers will be over this afternoon to help thee." She looked at Hannah with her eyes twinkling and winked. "With eight men in the family, no one gets worked too hard at our house. I'm the one with no one to help in the kitchen."

Hannah helped Mrs. Olsen into the buggy, climbed in herself, and started down the road with Jonathan riding his pony along side.

Back at the Haviland farm, Hannah finished her chores and doubled up doing the chores that Aaron normally would have done. The cow was bawling to be milked by the time she got to the barn.

Jonathan went to work on the plowing while Mrs. Olsen tended to Mrs. Haviland upstairs. Hannah cleaned the kitchen, prepared some sandwiches that she took down to Jonathan for lunch and then took a tray up to Mrs. Olsen.

Jonathan's mother took the tray from Hannah at the door to the bedroom and thanked her for the lunch. She went back inside to put the tray on a table, by a rocker, and then came back to the door where Hannah waited. She held up the start of a white baby afghan she was crocheting.

Hannah spent the rest of the afternoon doing her mother's chores: baking bread, making a pie, sweeping the house, cooking a chicken for supper and tending to the basket of never-ending mending.

By the time the old grandfather clock chimed five, Mrs. Olsen came down stairs to "stretch her legs," as she said to Hannah. She sat in the old rocker by the kitchen stove while Hannah scurried to set the table, then brought the chicken, potatoes and vegetables to the table. Granted she was tired, but on the other hand she was proud of herself to have accomplished so much.

When Hannah started to go get Jonathan, Mrs. Olsen tut-tutted and went out onto the back porch with a skillet and a metal spoon. She banged and banged and then when satisfied that Jonathan had heard, she came back inside and admired the spread of food.

"The boys are always listening for my special bell," she explained to Hannah. "Those eight men can half a side of beef in one sitting. It's a mite nice to have thee to wait on me for a change. I could get spoiled very quickly."

Sure enough, Jonathan came in the back door a few minutes later and quickly washed his hands at the sink.

They made quick work of the food. Mrs. Olsen yawned, stretched and pushed herself away from the table with a groan, and said it was time for her to go back upstairs.

"Thee is a wonderful cook, Hannah. I could use thee at my house if thy mother would let us adopt thee." She chuckled at her own joke as she trudged toward the stairs. "It won't be much longer now. My estimation is that thee will have a new brother or sister by morning."

Jonathan went out to finish his work in the fields while Hannah put the food away and cleaned the kitchen one more time. It was completely dark by the time they both finished their work so they could sit on the back steps and eat a piece of pie. It was the one that Hannah had made and she realized that the crust was not light and fluffy like her mother's. However, Jonathan didn't notice. He ate the first slice in three bites and ate a second in two mouthfuls.

Hannah, who was so used to being on her own, wondered how it would be to have nine people in the family. She found herself talking freely with him, sharing her experiences about the slave, Elijah. She even confessed her dreams to him and wondered out loud if there were indeed two little slave girls on their way to find their father.

"He told me that his two daughters were coming too. He sent them a message and expected to see them. Mama says they must have been sold to a neighboring plantation and had to make their own escape. I'm not even sure that they exist. He was very confused with his fever and all." She thought a moment and bit her lip. "He was never really well when he kept mentioning them. I promised him that I would try to help find them. But if they are real, I wouldn't know how to start to find them."

She was surprised how easy it was to talk to Jonathan and his mother. She felt she was losing some of her shyness with them. They were such a friendly family.

"I don't know either, "said Jonathan, filling his mouth with a huge bite from his third piece of pie. "I guess we need to keep our eyes and ears open."

She looked at him in amazement. "Does thee mean that thee would help me find out if there are two slave girls looking for their father?"

"Of course." Jonathan insisted, looking serious for once. "I think that someone in Braytown would know if there are two slave girls on the run, if anyone knows. Mama always goes there to visit the free Negroes to take food and help with their birthings. We can go with her next time and ask around."

Hannah was elated.

The next morning, while gathering eggs, Hannah heard the faint cry of a baby coming from the house. She and Jonathan had been up early to start their chores. She was so excited that she almost dropped the basket. She even patted Bitty in a friendly way, while the ornery hen gave her a mean look with narrowed eyes.

She ran to the kitchen, mindful of the fragile eggs, washed her hands and ran for the stairs. She zipped up the steps, two at a time.

Mrs. Olsen let her into the bedroom and there was her mother holding a tiny baby, who almost disappeared in the folds of a the white blanket Mrs. Olson had made.

Hannah came close and grinned at her mother.

"Say hello to thy sister, Hannah. Meet Elizabeth Rose. We decided to name her after Daniel's mother." Hannah bent down to peer at the baby who had a shock of red hair. Hannah was delighted at the sight of the little creature.

"Hello, baby sister. I'm thy big sister, Hannah. Pleased to make thy acquaintance." She made a little curtsey. Mrs. Olsen and her mother laughed. Hannah giggled. The baby's eyes fluttered a little but she soon fell back asleep.

"She's tired, poor dear. She worked hard to be born." Her mother said. Mrs. Olsen was bustling through the bedroom picking up linens for the wash. "Seems like thee both worked hard this morning," she said with a tired smile. " I will be getting Jonathan from the field to fetch me some water and help me start the laundry. I'll be in the yard if thee needs me. Hannah keep thy mother company for a while. I've got work to do."

Soon they heard the banging of the spoon on the frying pan and within five minutes, mother and daughter heard the hoof beats of Jonathan's horse as he came back from the field to help his mother start the fire to heat the water in the big cauldron for the wash.

Hannah's hand itched to sketch the scene with her mother and the new sister. But she had no paper. What to do?

Then she remembered the daffodil picture on the mantle. She ran downstairs, grabbed her picture and a pencil and hurried back up stairs to her parent's bedroom

She barely sat on the chair near the bed, and began sketching furiously. Almost as if she was afraid she would forget something if she didn't get started right away.

"I want to draw thee right now, Mama. I have to. Can I? Please?"

Mrs. Haviland laughed. "Yes, thee may. After all it's a celebration for a wonderful, healthy baby."

Hannah soon moved from the chair to the bottom of the bed and continued her sketching. Finally she was finished.

She held the finished portrait up for her mother to see. Her mother was astonished at how quickly Hannah had captured the scene within a few minutes.

"God has certainly talented thee, daughter."

Hannah could hardly wait until Friday to add the color needed to bring the picture to life.

Things would go well as long as the bounty hunters stayed away; as long as her father made it safely to the doctor; as long as Elijah got well; and as long as she and Jonathan could find the two runaway slave girls and reunite them with their father.

Rumors

The bounty hunters did come again, the very next morning while Mrs. Olsen and Jonathan were still there.

Hannah was the one who opened the front door at the insistent knocking. She looked into the face of the sheriff and saw the familiar crowd of rough men behind him, urging him to open the screen door and push by her.

Hannah made a grab for the screen door and pulled it shut with a click. She put a finger to her lips and whispered, "Shhhh. My mother's just had her baby and they are both asleep. Please don't come in and disturb them. We have no slaves here. My mother already told thee that when thee were here last."

The men looked at one another in confusion. They were used to people stepping aside in fear and they seemed unsure what to do with a young girl who didn't seem to be afraid of them.

Hannah had done all she could do at that point. She hollered for Mrs. Olsen, who came running from the kitchen with a rolling pin, covered with flour from pie making.

She moved Hannah behind her and faced the sheriff herself through the screen.

"Ya gonna hit me with that rolling pin, Mrs. Olsen?" the sheriff asked as he took in the small, round woman with the fierce look on her face. "I thought you Quakers set store by being peaceable like?" He reached for the door handle and made to bring himself and the others inside.

Mrs. Olsen chuckled and put her empty hand on the door to keep it shut.

"Goodness, sheriff. Thee caught me in the midst of making a passel of apple pies. Doesn't thee know that Mrs. Haviland here just had her baby and all that shuffling and shouting that thee are doing is bound to wake the dead. As was said before, there's no slave hidden on this property, so I'm asking thee kindly to go away and leave us in peace. There are only four women in the house and a boy plowing the field. Doesn't seem to me that, that's anything to threaten anyone. Why doesn't thee go look for thy runaways somewhere else?"

At the doubtful look on the sheriff's face, Mrs. Olsen added. "There's no runaway hereabouts. I promise on my Bible. If I had it here," she added under her breath. Hannah grinned and hid it behind her hand.

"Now just a minute, Mrs. Olsen. Hold on, ma'am. Not so fast. This time we've gotten word that two young female slaves crossed the river at Mayville last night. We're looking for them. They're from a very rich plantation and they're worth a thousand dollars to these here men. You wouldn't be hiding some young girls now would you? With all the women folk here today?"

Hannah couldn't see Mrs. Olsen's eyes, but she suspected that they were not twinkling now. "Sheriff, I have given thee my solemn oath. Surely thee would not think that I am lying to thee? I'm sure that's an interesting tale about the escaped slaves, but I have told thee that there are no slaves here, male or female. Is there anything else thee wanted? No? Well feel free take as much water as thee needs for thy horses as you leave."

The sheriff backed up a step, unsure what to do, yet again. Hannah could see that he hated to give in to this little woman. Finally he gave up, turned, yelled to the men behind him that they were going to search the grounds again, and amidst the grumbling, the men left the porch.

Mrs. Olsen shut the wooden door with a sigh and clicked the lock.

Hannah ran to the kitchen and spied through the screen door and heard the men arguing among themselves. Several went boldly into the barn and searched. Some checked out the springhouse. She heard the chickens squawking as men prowled through the chicken coop. When they met again in the yard, all shook their heads at the others that there was no one there. They soon left the yard at a gallop in a spray of gravel and dust.

When Hannah turned back to the kitchen, Mrs. Olsen was attacking the pie dough with a vengeance. Tonight the pie would be cherry. "Good riddance," she said under her breath.

That evening sitting on the back porch, under the stars with Jonathan while they ate their pie (a custom which seemed to have become a nightly ritual after the chores were done) Hannah brought up what the bounty hunters had said about the two girl slaves crossing the river.

"He said they crossed last night. How will the girls know which house their father went to? How will they find him? How will we find them?"

"I still think that we should go to Braytown with Mama and ask around. People down there trust the Quakers. They know that our Meeting House will help the slaves escape to Canada. Maybe they know something."

"I think there is something else we can do."

"What?" Jonathan asked as he swiped hair out of his eyes. "What else can we do?"

"We can find them ourselves. By tracking." She knew Jonathan and his brothers tracked game for food. " Wouldn't tracking two girls through the woods be easier than an animal?"

Hannah was warming up to the topic. "I know all the Olsen boys are expert hunters. What if thee and I track them down?" She shrugged her shoulders. "We can find clues, footprints, scraps of cloth. We could check the woods near the crossing at Mayville? We could ask the families at the Meeting House?"

Jonathan didn't look convinced.

"Thee knows what the elders think about the children getting involved with the Underground

Railroad. They would frown on it. Beside, doesn't thee think the bounty hunters are good trackers."

Hannah ignored his question in her rush to explain her plan.

"Once we found them we could turn them over to the elders. They're out there somewhere, looking for their father and I think they're lost and hiding somewhere. We have to help them. Besides that, I promised." She waited a beat. "What does thee think?"

"Well," Jonathan looked at her, " we could at least find out all the information we can. I can see that thee are very worried about these girls." Jonathan said with compassion. " I will help thee if I can. " He took another bite of his second piece of pie. "Why are they so important to thee?"

Hannah tried to put her feelings into words. "I tried to imagine if that were me out there. Eleven years old. Running for my life. I know I would be so afraid. I would pray that God would send someone who would want to help me."

There was a hitch in her voice as she tried not to cry. She thought about the absolute terror of being on the run knowing those bounty hunters were right on thy heels like a dog treeing a raccoon.

Mrs. Olsen came out onto the porch then and sent them upstairs to bed. Another long day was ahead.

After kissing her mother and sister good night, Hannah tucked herself into bed and sent up a prayer for Goodness and Mercy, for that was what she had begun calling them in her mind since she didn't really know their given names. Her one last thought, before sleep crept upon her, was that maybe Mrs. Olsen could help her think of ideas. Her own mother could be help, but she was busy right now with Elizabeth and Hannah was sure she didn't have the time for her daydreaming daughter's ideas.

The next morning over breakfast, Mrs. Olsen told Jonathan and Hannah that they were going to return to school today. Hannah had lost track of the days, but was excited when she realized that today was Friday. She wanted to take her sketch to school and use the watercolors to finish the portrait that she had made of her mother and Elizabeth.

Hannah related her anxiety to Mrs. Olsen about the two slave girls and asked what she thought they could do to help.

Mrs. Olsen seemed really interested in the fate of the two girls, but she cautioned, "Thee doesn't really know if these two girls, mentioned by the bounty hunters, are the daughters of Elijah, does thee?"

"No, but it seems like a strange coincidence it they weren't."

"True enough," Mrs. Olsen acknowledged. "Tomorrow's Saturday. If thee ride over to my house at eight, the three of us will go into town to the store. Maybe we will hear some news about the two runaways. Rumors are always circulating at the general store."

Hannah was happy with that idea.

Art Class

Afternoon recess was finally over and the art class started in spite of Hannah's impatience. She had been absent-minded all day in the reading, math and history classes. Every time Miss Perkins called on her, her mind was either wandering to think of her sketch or the two runaway girls.

When she went to the front to get the watercolors, Hannah suddenly changed her mind and chose instead, the oil pastel sticks. They were like sticks of chalk but brightly colored. She wanted to use something darker for the picture today. Miss Perkins cautioned that they were messy and might stain her dress. "Take care with them now." Hannah looked at her drab black dress and thought that if any pastel got on her dress, it wouldn't show up. That was one advantage to always wearing black.

Hannah deliberately made the colors light so that the bed and bed linens were a washed out blue/green. The only dash of color was the red color she used to capture the auburn highlights of her mother and sister's hair.

Miss Perkins was busy helping the younger girls down in the front of the classroom, who were fussing over what they wanted to sketch. Half the period was gone and they hadn't settled on anything that they wanted to draw. The youngest student, Molly Hawkins, started crying out of frustration. She was barely six years old and still occasionally cried in the afternoon for her mother. Miss Perkins spent her time patting Molly and trying to reassure her to keep trying.

Hannah colored on, lost in her visions of how the colors should blend together. Her tongue was caught between her teeth as she colored and smudged the colors with her fingers to get the pastels to just the right shade.

Finally with the young ones settled, Miss Perkins found the time to wander around the older students' seats and look over their shoulders at the variety of work that was being done.

She paused behind Hannah.

"Oh Hannah," she breathed reverently. "This is absolutely lovely. You have such talent." At the compliment, other girls crowded around to see the picture.

Soon the girls, who ignored her most recesses and lunch times, were asking her questions about her drawing and her new baby sister. Some of them wanted to know if Hannah would make sketches of them and sell it to them as presents for their parents.

Miss Perkins laughed. "Hannah, you already have people offering to pay for your services. After you graduate, I'd love to be able to send you back to New York to my former art teacher. Why I even think you would be good enough to go to Paris to study."

Jonathan came up behind Hannah, to watch over her shoulder. She was starting to get a little shy with all the attention she was getting.

"Thee could go to Paris, Hannah." He stopped and cleared his throat, "If the country does not go to war. Papa says it's only a matter of time before the South secedes and we go to war. There's talk everywhere about it."

That comment made everyone uncomfortable and soon everyone drifted back to his or her desks.

After school, Hannah was at the pump, trying to scrub the chalk off her hands without much success. Since the pastels were oily the water wasn't helping much. Jonathan rode up on his pony and watched Hannah struggling with the mess on her hands. He tossed her a handkerchief. "Here use this. I think thee is better off with soap." It was better than nothing, so Hannah accepted. She scraped the mess off her hands as best she could until she could get some soap at home. She decided that she was sticking to watercolors from now on.

"Thee might like to take a detour with me before you go home. It won't take long." As she looked up inquiringly, he added, "Some of the boys at lunch were talking about a wanted poster posted by the Mayville ferry dock. They said it had a picture of two little girls who were wanted as runaway slaves. Interested?"

Luckily Hannah had ridden Princess today, since she hadn't had to leave her behind for Aaron.

She couldn't ride fast enough. She jumped on her horse and pushed Princess into a gallop as soon as they cleared the schoolyard fence, never letting Jonathan catch up with her until she skidded to a stop at the ferry dock.

The ferry was on the far side as they dismounted and ran to the tree to see the wanted poster. Two crudely drawn pictures showed the faces of the two twins. They looked smaller than Hannah although Elijah had said that they were her age. The artist had made their eyes look wide and frightened. Hannah bent close so she could read the small print. Jonathan read over her shoulder.

WANTED
$1,000 REWARD

FOR THE CAPTURE
&
RETURN OF TWO
FEMALE SLAVES
ANSWERING TO THE
NAMES
SUKEY AND SADIE
CONTACT OVERSEER AT
LEVILLE PLANTATION

LEXINGTON, KENTUCKY

Hannah's heart stopped. She was sure these were Elijah's children. This was Goodness and Mercy. How would they find them? Where could they be hiding?

She reached out and ripped the poster off the tree and folded it and put it in her pocket.

The ferryman, just pulling his barge into the dock, saw her and gave a holler. "Don't be ripping them there posters down. They's public property." He gave her a glare. She gave him one right back and hopped back on her horse, all thoughts of art gone out of her head. She only had thoughts of rescuing the two girls on the wanted posters.

"I'm going to find your parents," the ferryman promised, " and you two will be in trouble."

"That'll be hard," Jonathan, laughed as he and Hannah raced back down the road to their homes. "We look like all the other Quakers." Hannah laughed at that thought. Jonathan continued, " We need to give that poster to Mama. It can't be a coincidence now."

That evening, Mrs. Haviland brought the baby down to the parlor where Hannah was trying to catch up on the mending in her mother's sewing basket.

"Here Hannah. Thee can hold Elizabeth while I do this mending. I declare. I feel so lazy just having the baby to care for. Mrs. Olsen spoiled me rotten." Hannah moved to the rocker while her mother deposited the small bundle, that was her sister, into her arms. She pulled down the corner of the blanket and saw her sister's bright blue eyes looking at her.

"She's awake!" Hannah was surprised.

"She will be asleep soon if thee rocks her," Hannah's mother said as she began pulling her husband's holey sock over the darning ball and began to sew.

Mrs. Haviland glanced up at her two daughters and smiled proudly. Hannah's chair rocked and squeaked occasionally. Her mother quickly noticed the portrait propped on the mantle. She gave a small sound of pleasure. "Hannah, thy picture of Elizabeth and me is exceptionally good. Thee got the colors just right."

Hannah looked up from the now-sleeping baby, pleased with her mother's praise.

"I've decided never to use pastels again. They're too messy. I think I'll stick with the watercolors. Miss Perkins said that I was good enough to go to New York or Paris to study art."

Mrs. Haviland frowned. "Yes, dear. Thy artwork is very good, but I fear that war will come first. It seems to be coming faster now no matter how much we pray for peace."

Trip to the General Store

On Saturday, the general store in Aberdeen was crowded with customers stocking up on supplies. "I'm going to see about some material for Mr. Olsen's shirts," Mrs. Olsen said to Hannah. "Thee and Jonathan can look around while thee waits for me." She headed straight for the bolts of shirting cloth.

Hannah drifted over to the shelf that held boxes of pencils and pads of lined school paper. She wished the store would carry colored pencils like Miss Perkins had at school. She wandered over to the checker game near the pot bellied stove and watched two old men play on a board balanced on a barrel head. The two men were arguing more than they were moving their checkers. They were discussing the newly elected president, Mr. Lincoln.

"His abolitionist ways is going to push us into war. You mark my words," the bald headed man said and to emphasize his point he spit a stream of tobacco juice into a spittoon near his boots. "Let sleeping dogs lie, I say. Let the South do what they want. 's no skin offen our noses. If people want to own slaves, then so be it."

The other checker player harrumphed and puffed on his pipe until blue smoke wreathed around his head. Hannah coughed as it drifted over to her. At least her big, black bonnet kept some of the smoke away. The man with the pipe took it from his mouth and pointed at Hannah with the stem of it.

"Them there Quakers is working hard to hide the runaways and get them to Canada. Isn't that right little Quaker girl?" His voice wasn't kind. "Do your parents hide slaves?" he asked pointedly, laughing at her as others looked on.

Hannah was saved from replying when Mrs. Olsen's hand snaked down on her arm and pulled her away from the checkerboard.

"Come along now Hannah, dear. Thee needs to look at this material with me."

Hannah felt her face get hot as Mrs. Olsen dragged her to the other side of the store. She felt like all eyes in the shop were looking at her. Quakers were always looked upon as odd. Hannah had heard of Quaker men getting beat up on the streets of New York for making such an issue against slavery. Many felt, as did these checker players, that the South and slavery should just be ignored. In 1861 most people were afraid of war.

Mrs. Olsen pulled out a bolt of white cotton and pulled one end of the material out to the tip of her right fingers. She then turned her face to the left and stretched the fabric to touch the end of her nose.

Hannah knew that was how farmwives estimated a yard of material. Mrs. Olsen studied the price.

"Shirts for Mr. Olsen and Adam will take about three yards. If thee can wait here, I'll go get Mr. Hatcher to cut me some from this bolt."

Hannah fingered the colored cloth on the bolts of material for dresses and felt a hint of guilt. She was ashamed of herself that she hated her black clothes. Hadn't Jonathan said that the blacks trusted those people who wore the Quaker clothes? And hadn't the ferryman been unable to see who they were because of the black clothes. And what about the pastels? The color of her dress made it nearly impossible to make her dress dirty. Maybe there were some good benefits to wearing these drab colors. But still, she was attracted to the bright bolts of cloth.

Feed sacks were stacked near the window. Hannah's mother used the flannel-like material from the feed sacks, once they were empty, to make nightgowns, underwear and petticoats. Once the material was washed, it was soft to the touch.

Some of the poorer girls in town had school dresses made out of that kind of material since it was so cheap. Only a few rich women could afford to buy their clothes off the rack in the general store.

Hannah felt herself drawn back to the pencils, but one look at Mrs. Olsen's face as she ventured back toward the front of the store, sent her scurrying outside.

On the porch of the general store, she drifted over to the steps where she could hear the conversation Jonathan was having with some boys from school. She bent down and petted a stray cat that lived in the blacksmith's barn so that it wouldn't be obvious that she was spying on the boys.

Jonathan was well liked by the boys at school. His sense of humor and his ready smile made him popular in spite of his strange Quaker clothes and beliefs.

"Hello, Pretty. What's your name?" Hannah asked as she petted the friendly tabby. Her fur was soft to the touch and she seemed well cared for. The cat purred and strutted to get her neck scratched while Hannah listened in on the interesting conversation going on not ten feet from her.

"I swear it, Jonathan," Lyle Weaver insisted. "I saw them. There's ghosts haunting Brect's Island." Lyle's hair stood out in little tufts all over his head like he had just rolled out of bed, although it was the afternoon. He was warming up to his story.

" My pa and I went hunting over there 'cause Pa said he saw an eight-point buck there and wanted to kill it. That dang buck was cussed enough to keep going through those woods and led us a merry chase. That's when we seen them." The other boys listening egged him on. "What'd you see?" the Collins boy asked. "Tell us again."

"The ghosts that's what. We still hadn't shot that old buck. It had gotten dark and all of a sudden we seen lights in the trees and people in white robes floating high up in the trees. My pa said they was angels, but I knew he was scared cause they was ghosts. We ran out of them woods and hightailed it back to our boat and home."

"Where on Brect's Island?" Jonathan asked.

"Near the crossing from the Mayville Road. Was right spooky."

Hannah chuckled to herself as the freckles on Lyle's face stood out in sharp relief. He seemed to be torn between fright and bragging and didn't know which way to go.

Hannah thought the ghosts could be the runaway girls, Goodness and Mercy. But why would they give their hiding place away using lanterns and wearing white robes? There had to be another explanation.

Mrs. Olsen called to them from across the road. She was piling her purchases into the Olsen's buggy. When Hannah caught up with her she had the reins in her hands and was ready to go. Jonathan and Hannah scrambled aboard as Mrs. Olsen clucked to the horse.

Hannah noticed that they were going in the opposite direction from their homes. Jonathan asked first. "Where are we going now, Mama?"

106

Mrs. Olsen replied. "I thought we'd go visit Braytown and ask around about the two girls. Maybe we will find that they turned up there safely. It's easy enough for runaways to hide out there." Hannah was glad that Mrs. Olsen was interested in finding out what had happened to the two girls.

Braytown was a settlement of free blacks. Folks in Braytown were used to bounty hunters coming there searching for runaways. It was situated just north of a six-mile stretch of wilderness that had once been leveled by a tornado. The resulting damage of miles of twisted trees and swamplands was the perfect place for slaves to hide. Multitudes of slaves were able to lose themselves in the debris. Even tracking dogs wouldn't go in there, it was so tangled.

Free blacks had emigrated there in 1826 from North Carolina. They had drained the north end of the six-mile stretch, the boggy land that no one else wanted. They hauled dirt, plowed it and planted it. They made it work for them. However, they left the southern miles of swamp untouched so that their brothers and sisters fleeing from the south would have a place to hide from the trackers.

When the runaways finally made it to Braytown, the free blacks hid them until they could pass them off to the Quakers, for the long trip to Canada. It was because of this that the blacks in Braytown welcomed the arrival of the Quakers. They were partners in the running of the Underground Railroad.

As the trap drove down the main street of Braytown, children who had been playing in the street began running along side the buggy, laughing. "We can go see Friend Eunice," Mrs. Olsen explained. We always work with her family when we have runaways to hide."

Friend Eunice was a tall black woman with a colorful turban tied around her head, hiding her hair. Hannah noticed her large white smile and her friendly eyes. Hannah had to smile back.

Eunice was holding a baby that looked newborn to Hannah and was holding the hand of a toddler who had on a miniature version of her mother's turban. Her eyes were wide and curious but she hid most of her body behind her mother.

"Friend Eunice," Mrs. Olsen said as she motioned for Jonathan to tie up the horse. She got down out of the buggy and shook hands with the black woman. "How are thee this fine day?'

Jonathan quickly tied the horse to the porch railing while Mrs. Olsen and Hannah went up the steps. Eunice opened the front door and welcomed them into the small cabin. It was darker inside than Hannah was used to because there were no windows

109

to let in light. Inside, the cabin was simple and small. Only one room. There was a table and four chairs in front of a large fireplace. Other than the bed in the corner and a small wooden cradle, there was no other furniture to be seen.

The guests were directed to sit at the table while the black woman took the fourth chair.

Mrs. Olsen explained the story of Elijah and his belief that his two girls were looking for him. She pulled the wanted poster out of her pocket and smoothed it out on the table in front of the black woman. "We think this is a poster about Elijah's girls. Do you know if they have showed up in Braytown?"

Eunice squinted to look at the paper as if she needed glasses.

"I can't read them words, Miz Olsen, but there ain't been no talk about no girls taking shelter in

Braytown. Those slave hunters already been by here twice now. They done busted up the preacher's house 'cause they couldn't find no trace of the girls."

Hannah remembered the violence she had felt from the bounty hunters who came to her door twice already. If the Havilands had been black, would the bounty hunters have pushed their way in and busted up their house when they couldn't find any runaways?

Her heart fell when she realized that the two girls were missing somewhere between the river and Braytown.

When Jonathan was sent out to the buggy to fetch a basket of food for Eunice's family, Hannah related the story she had overheard in town about the strange sights on Brect's Island.   None of them could imagine what it was that Lyle Weaver and his father had seen.

The mystery only made Hannah more determined to find out the truth.

Papa's Return

Hannah heard the clattering of Papa's wagon Sunday morning. The sound carried into her bedroom and woke her up.

It was still dark outside, so Hannah knew it was early. The two men weren't even trying to be quiet.

Hannah jumped out of bed, pulled on her wrapper over her nightgown and dashed barefoot downstairs, through the kitchen and out the back door. She let it bang but she didn't care. Her mother must have heard the noise and would be getting up too.

Her papa and her brother were home. That's all that mattered. And they were safe. She had been so afraid for them.

She threw herself into her father's arms and started talking so fast about the new baby, the bounty hunters and the lost girls that her words tumbled over each other and made no sense.

"Wait! Wait!" her father said. "Hannah, I can't take it all in. Thee must settle down. Tell me when I am finished with the horses. They traveled all night and they need food and rest."

He put Hannah down. The dew was cold on her feet but she didn't care. The two men went back to unhitching the team and then leading them into the barn for a rubdown and some food.

Hannah stood still on the grass until her father came back. She was so glad to see them home that she was in a state of shock. Her brother walked by and gave her a wink and ruffled her hair. "Hey Freckle face. Where are thy shoes?"

Aaron laughed at her as her father scooped her up again and hugged her tightly. "So we have a new babe in our family. I didn't catch the name."

"It's Elizabeth Rose after Grandma Haviland. She's got red hair like Mama." Mr. Haviland laughed at that news. "Oh, no," he said teasing Hannah. "We're in trouble now with two red heads in the family." Hannah giggled.

Mrs. Haviland indeed was up, dressed and starting breakfast. She kissed her husband and hugged her son tightly, then went back to work, cutting the bacon slab into strips and frying them.

She turned to Hannah. "Run quickly dear and gather some fresh eggs. We are having a celebration breakfast."

Hannah ran. With father and Aaron back home things felt like they were back to normal again and her troubles seemed far away.

Over breakfast father told all about the trip north and how the slave trackers blocked many of the roads. They had to take back roads much of the time.

"Once they searched the wagon," he said. "But Aaron and I had seen the roadblock in the distance, so we carried Elijah into the woods and hid him, then we double backed after we passed the road block and picked him back up. It was our only close call."

Aaron was on his third helping of food. "I missed thy cooking Mama. No one makes food like thee. I like to have starved." "Yes, I can see that," Mrs. Haviland laughed as she looked at her healthy son.

116

"We finally decided to travel at night and sleep by day. Thanks to the directions the elders gave us, we found Quakers all along the way that helped us. All in all we had a good trip. We found the doctor and Elijah was sitting up, his fever gone by the time we started out for home." Mr. Haviland said.

"Thank the Lord," said Mrs. Haviland.

Papa said to his daughter. "Tell me about the bounty hunters." At the mention of them, Hannah excitedly told him about the two visits they had made to the house. She also told how they had visited the Olsen's house and Eunice's house in Braytown.

"Eunice said they busted up the preacher's house because they were so angry that they didn't find anyone."

Hannah also filled her dad and brother in on the wanted poster and what Elijah had said to her before he made the trip north.

"Jonathan, Mrs. Olsen and I think that the girls in the wanted poster are Elijah's children. If we find them, will they be able to find their father?"

Hannah waited anxiously for her father to answer. It would be a problem if the girls came to the Havilands and still couldn't find their father.

"Yes, Hannah. They will be able to find him. Aaron and I will drive them north and the Underground will know where Elijah went. We will make sure that they are reunited."

The family soon got ready for church. It would be the first time that the new baby would go with the family. Mrs. Haviland wrapped Elizabeth in the new blanket that Mrs. Olsen had crocheted. There would be many prayers of thanksgiving today for the healthy new baby.

Later that evening, Hannah showed her father the picture of the daffodils she had painted and the portrait of her mother and sister. She had to explain what pastels were when he asked what she had colored the picture with. Her father was pleased. "It's a shame that these two pictures are back to back. I can build thee a frame, but which one will thee want to be showing?"

It was a hard decision. Her mother and father were quiet while she made up her mind. She finally settled on the mother and baby picture, although it was a hard choice. The daffodils would have to stay hidden.

By Monday, everyone in the household was back to their regular schedule again and the thoughts of the two runaway slaves was almost forgotten by Hannah until Jonathan reminded her at lunchtime.

She was eating by herself again. The small burst of popularity she had gained over her drawing had disappeared. Jonathan walked up and sat next to her on the wall. He was fanning himself with his hat. It was a hot day and he had been running playing dodge ball with all the boys.

"I have an idea about the two slave girls. Did thee ride thy pony today?"

"No. I had to leave him for Aaron."

Jonathan frowned.

"Thee will just have to ride behind me, then."

"Where are we going?"

"I want to go back down to the ferry dock. I have some questions for the ferryman. Does thee want to go?"

"Of course. I just hope the ferryman doesn't recognize us from the day we took the poster."

"He won't. Trust me. Most people think we all look alike."

"What kind of questions do thee have?"

"Thee will see," he answered mysteriously.

After school they almost ran out of the schoolhouse to where Jonathan's horse, Checkers, was tied. Jonathan said that the horse's coat looked like patches of squares on a checkerboard.

They wasted no time getting on the horse. Riding bareback was a little tricky for Hannah especially behind Jonathan. She had to hold on to him with one hand and keep her bonnet from flying off with the other. They were riding like the wind.

They finally arrived at the ferry dock and tied the horse to a tree where the old poster had been tacked. A new one replaced the one they had taken. Hannah was itching to take it down and rip it into a million pieces.

On the walk down to the dock, Jonathan told her what he had been thinking.

"Remember Lyle's story? I think the things they saw that they thought were ghosts were really the girls or something the girls were doing to scare people away. Once it gets around that the island has ghosts, no one will go there to hunt anymore."

Hannah admitted that the story Lyle Weaver told was hard to believe. "But I did think that somehow it might be the two girls also. I just can't explain the lights and the ghost creatures."

"I can't either. But it's the only place left for us to look. Everything else we've tried is a dead end."

Jonathan pulled Hannah along behind him as he walked boldly down to the ferry. "Excuse me mister," he hollered to the man on the ferry. The man looked up and then climbed out onto the dock and began walking toward them.

Hannah was relieved that the man wasn't the same one that had seen them take the wanted poster. She breathed a sigh of relief. This ferryman was an older boy near the age of her brother. He was smiling as he came toward them.

"How can I help you two?" he asked as he stopped in front of them. "Ya' all need a ride to the other side of the river? Not too busy right now. Can have ya over there in two shakes of a lamb's tail."

Hannah heard the southern accent and decided that he was from the Kentucky side of the river.

"No thanks, all the same," Jonathan said. "I've just got some questions for thee. Does thee ever take passengers over to Brect's Island?"

"The island?" He turned and looked at the island out in the middle of the river, then looked back at them. He took off his hat and scratched his head while he thought. "Don't rightly know. Nobody ever asked to go over there before while I was working here."

Jonathan still wasn't done. "How much would thee charge to take the two of us over to the island, then fetch us back later?"

He thought on it for a minute. "I'd have to charge ya two cents for the two of you, over and back. I could do it anytime. Just show up and if I'm not busy I'll carry ya over."

"Thanks," Jonathan said. Hannah was dying to ask what his plan was but she wisely kept quiet until the boy walked back to the ferry.

Once they were out of earshot, Jonathan told her what he was thinking.

"If we can get 2 cents, we can both go over to the island and look around. We can leave a note for the girls explaining how to get to your farm."

"What if they can't read?" Hannah asked, thinking of what Eunice said about not being able to read.

Jonathan frowned. He hadn't thought of that problem.

"So how can we leave a message so they can understand if they can't read?" Jonathan asked.

"I don't know," Hannah admitted.

All the way back to the Haviland farm, Jonathan and Hannah were silent, trying to think of a plan. But they came up with nothing.

The Answer

By morning recess the next day, Hannah had come up with an idea. She told Jonathan about it while the other children played tag back and forth across the field. There was much yelling and screaming as almost everyone in the whole school was playing.

They sat on their usual spot on the stonewall. Jonathan listened quietly to Hannah's plan.

"Well, we don't know if they can read or not. But if we draw them a map with pictures instead of words, they may be able to follow that."

"I don't know…" Jonathan said. He frowned and took of his hat and started fanning his face. He had been running in the game a while ago and he was getting too hot in the black clothes.

"Look," Hannah said. She pulled a folded paper from her pocket. She had sketched out a map during spelling class, when they were supposed to be writing the spelling words ten times each.

Jonathan looked closely. She had drawn large, clear pictures to show the route to the Haviland's house. The map showed the island, the ferry dock, the left turn onto schoolhouse lane. It pictured the huge oak tree where the road forked and an excellent likeness of the front of the Haviland farmhouse. But the crowning touch of all was the pictures Hannah had drawn of herself and Jonathan in their black Quaker clothes. They were smiling and they were pointing to the area of the map where the Haviland house was.

There was an amazing likeness of Elijah in the bottom right hand corner of the map. He had his arms open as if he was welcoming his children.

128

Arrows tied it all together as they started at the island and showed the path to follow to get to safety. It was clever he thought. Very, very clever.

"This is amazing, Hannah." He was excited now. His smile stretched from ear to ear.

"Why did thee draw our picture too?" he asked.

Hannah chuckled. "So they wouldn't be afraid to follow the map. I guessed that they would have seen us on the island and would know that we only wanted to help them. Besides, they wouldn't be afraid of Quakers."

Jonathan gave her back the map. She folded it and tucked it back into her apron pocket.

Jonathan had another thought. "How will they get across the river?" Hannah thought a moment. "If they are on the island, they had to swim to get there. They'll get off the same way."

They made plans to visit the island early on Saturday morning. It was hard for Hannah to wait. Today was only Tuesday.

Exploring the Island

Saturday, after their chores were done, Hannah met Jonathan at his farm. They both had their ponies that day and they rode to the ferry dock together.

Between them, they had found 25 cents to pay for the ferry. They checked with the ferryman to see if he could take them over right then. It seemed to be a quiet time so he agreed.

Luckily it was the same ferryman that they had talked to on Monday. If the other man had been on duty, their plan would have failed.

The ferryman pushed off the barge with a long pole and starting from the front of the ferry, he put his shoulder into the pole and pushed and walked to the back of the boat. When he got there, he walked to the front with the pole and started over again.

Hannah was curious about something. "How deep is the water?" she asked him.

"Not too deep." Was the answer. "Maybe three feet. You could swim over if you wanted, but the water's icy cold."

The barge finally beached onto the edge of the island that was covered with gravel and small rocks. Jonathan and Hannah jumped off the front trying to miss the water on the rocks.

"What time shall I come back for you?" The ferryman asked.

"What time is it now?"

"Ten o'clock."

"Then pick us up at high noon. Two hours should be long enough for us to do what we need to do." Jonathan answered.

"Twelve it is." The ferryman answered as he pushed the boat off the beach. Hannah was thankful that he didn't seem at all curious as to why they wanted to go there.

Jonathan and Hannah began walking towards the center of the island, hoping to find some clues along the way.

When they felt they were in the middle of the woods, they began looking around for anything that might let them know that the girls were there.

They soon came across a circle of large stones that looked like it had once been a campfire. "Look at this Jonathan, " Hannah pointed to some of the ashes that were still glowing red. "Some of these are still hot."

Someone was on the island. Hopefully it was the two slave girls they were looking for. They looked around for about an hour but they found nothing more. They finally came back to the campfire.

Hannah took two nails out of her pocket and picked up a large rock. "I think we should leave the map here." She began hammering the map to the trunk of a big pine tree.

"That's a good place." Jonathan agreed.

All morning Hannah had been carrying her old lunch bucket with her. Now she sat it on the ground under the map. It was an empty syrup can that most school children used for carrying their lunches.

Jonathan watched her for a moment. "What is thee doing, Hannah." He was clearly confused.

"I brought some food for the girls. It must be hard to find food in this place."

"Good idea. Maybe that will make them want to trust us and follow the map."

134

By noon, the two were waiting on the beach when the ferryman arrived.

Soon they were back home, waiting for something to happen

Waiting

On Monday, it seemed that everyone was playing kick the can during lunch recess except Hannah who was sitting with two of the little first grade girls who were afraid to play. They sat on the stonewall that separated the schoolyard from the road, while they watched the action.

One person who was "it" put an old tin can in the middle of the field and then waited while one person, usually the best kicker in the school, kicked the can as far as he could. It usually was kicked into the woods to give everyone time to hide. While the children were hiding, the person who was "it" had to run as fast as he could to retrieve the can and put it back into the field in the original spot. As soon as "it" placed the can back in the field, he or she was free to go discover where everyone was hiding.

136

Hannah knew that the fun part of the game were the times that someone would run out of his or her hiding place and kick the can again, forcing the person who was "it" to try to race them to the can and tag the kicker before he could kick the can again.

If the person who was "it" tagged the kicker before he could reached the can, he or she would be out and have to stay in "prison" during the game. "Prison" was a large circle drawn in the dirt. Everyone who was caught had to stand in the circle. If someone, running out of the woods to kick the can, was tagged before he or she could kick the can, they had to stay in prison. If the one running out of the woods to kick the can was successful in kicking the can, before they were tagged, everyone in the prison would be free to hide again.

Hannah knew the rules by heart but she was reluctant to play because she wasn't a very fast runner. Besides there was her shyness. But she enjoyed sitting on the sidelines telling the little girls with her what was happening.

As usual, Clarence was chosen to be "it". No one liked him much and he usually got stuck with being "it" because majority ruled. Jonathan was usually elected as the kicker since he could make the can sail deep into the woods and distract Clarence until even the slowest could hide.

With the kick and with the can soaring across the field, the girls screamed and the boys bellowed and everyone ran for their favorite hiding places. The little girls on the wall with Hannah, Jane, Mary and Stephanie, squealed and clapped their hands as the game began.

Miss Perkins came out and sat with Hannah and watched the action going on it the meadow. She leaned over and whispered in Hannah's ear, "What's happening?" Hannah proceeded to tell her how the game was played. Hannah was very surprised that Miss Perkins sat on the dusty wall with them in her nice spring dress. It was a cheerful turquoise with dozens of little yellow ribbons trimming the neckline and hem.

After about ten minutes into the game, when Jonathan sneaked out of the woods and kicked the can again and freed the hostages in the dirt circle, Hannah felt the wall beneath her begin to shake. She didn't know what was happening. Then with the shaking came a sound like thunder. She looked at Miss Perkins with alarm. Miss Perkins rose and walked over to stand at the gate that was at the front of the schoolyard, just a few feet from where Hannah and the little girls were sitting. Miss Perkins was looking left down the road.

The thundering noise and the shaking ground was caused by a huge group of men galloping toward the school. A swirling cloud of dust from the dry road surrounded Hannah, the girls, and Miss Perkins. Everyone started coughing. It was the bounty hunters and the sheriff was at the front of the pack. Hannah assumed that they were looking for Goodness and Mercy. What if her map had made the girls come out of hiding and the bounty hunters found them today? Her stomach started churning with worry.

Suddenly the mass of thundering hooves slowed down so the mob of men could turn toward the schoolyard. A big, burly man with a red face and angry eyes arrived first and was out of his saddle, up to the gate, before Hannah could blink. He was in a hurry to do something. With a glare directed at Miss Perkins, he put his face down in her face. His voice

140

was a growl as he said, " We need to search this here schoolhouse."

"That's fine," said Miss Perkins smoothly. " It's a public building so I can't keep you out. But you won't find any slaves hiding there."

The men behind the burly man jumped off their horses and swarmed into the school like a bunch of angry bees looking for someone to sting. Frustrated with not finding anything there, they left the schoolhouse and began searching the meadow and the nearby woods. The kick the can players came out of hiding to see what was happening, then fearfully gathered around Miss Perkins and Hannah and the little girls still sitting on the wall. All the children watched the men's frantic search with terror in their eyes. None of the children understood the violence that seemed to motivate the men. Finally

Miss Perkins gathered up her skirts and marched over to the sheriff standing near the steps to the school.

"Sheriff. Enough! Our recess is over and we have to get back to our studies." She pointedly looked at the watch that was pinned to the bodice of her dress and clicked her tongue. "We are already behind in our afternoon studies." She looked at him crossly.

"Studies? Bah!" The beefy man with the red, angry face stood between the sheriff and the gate. He was so angry that he was almost choking on his words. "We're looking for two runaway slaves and if you have anything to do with hiding them…" His words trailed off angrily. He looked around like he wanted to hit something.

Hannah watched a blush rise and cover Miss Perkins's cheeks, a flush of anger. Still Miss Perkins ignored the sputtering man, directing her attention

142

and conversation to the sheriff. Miss Perkins remained polite and calm. Two of the tall boys, who were taller than Miss Perkins, and taller than most of the men standing by the horses, went over to stand beside her, one on each side, like bodyguards.

Most of the students who had come running up, still didn't know what was happening. Some of the little girls sitting on the wall with Hannah started crying softly. They were frightened. Cindy, standing nearby started the normal howling she did when she was upset.

Hannah noticed two dogs sitting in the dust near the feet of the horses. She assumed that they were tracking dogs and that they were used to sniffing out the scent of runaway slaves. Her stomach began aching as she pictured them tracking Goodness and Mercy. The realization frightened her. She sent a quick prayer to heaven for their safety.

In the meantime, the sheriff walked back to the gate, maybe to call it a day and have the men let the children get back to their studies. That's when the beefy bully noticed Hannah. He walked over to where she was still sitting on the wall and in a fit of temper reached down and scooped her off the wall and held her over the ground. Her feet were dangling. Her teeth clattered together as he began shaking her like a dog shakes a rope when someone is holding the other end.

She heard Jonathan yell, "Hey there." She could hear everyone talk at once. She could hear Cindy's howl get louder. Miss Perkins was yelling at the beefy man to let her down. Some of the bounty hunters were protesting his actions. At another time Hannah would have laughed at the chaos of noise, if she hadn't been so afraid of what the man was going to do to her.

He ignored the protests around him and shouted in Hannah's face.

"I bet this here Quaker girl knows more than she's telling. I bet she knows where those two slave girls are a hiding. Her kind is always hiding those runaways and helping them git to Canada."

He continued holding her up with one hand and shoved the tattered wanted poster into her face so she could see the frightened faces of Goodness and Mercy. It was like the poster she had stolen off the tree by the ferry dock.

"Ya know where they is don't ya?" he demanded, pushing the paper closer to her face. Hannah shook her head. She was getting angry. She could feel her temper giving her strength to talk. "No I don't but I wish I did. I'd make sure they escaped the likes of thee!"

The man yelled in frustration. Miss Perkins had run to where Hannah was dangling and snatched her away from the man's grasp. She set her down on the ground. "Are you all right?" She asked gently as she stood between Hannah and the bounty hunter.

Miss Perkins raised her voice louder than the din of shouting men, yelling students, crying tots and barking dogs. Hannah was the only silent one in the whole area.

"Sheriff, I demand that you make these" she struggled for the right word, "bounty hunters leave the premise right now or I will have one of the boys ride to get the president of the school board down here right now. People in this town will not allow children to be shoved around for any reason, you mark my words."

Evidently the sheriff heard her. He put two fingers in his mouth and gave a shrill whistle that had

Hannah and others clap their hands over their ears with the pain of the sound.

The cacophony stopped abruptly. Miss Perkins herded the children up the steps into the schoolroom. Hannah glanced back. The men were still angry and yelling but now they were fighting among themselves. The two tracking dogs were still barking. The horses, skittish from all the yelling, were stamping their hooves and blowing air through their nostrils. Some were shaking their bridles in nervousness as if they wanted to bolt

Inside, Miss Perkins seemed shaken. She slammed the big wooden door shut with a bang and threw the lock into place. She hurried around directing students into their desks, trying to get them involved in some schoolwork. All the students looked stricken and shocked all except the two older boys who had been Miss Perkins' bodyguards. They were standing in the aisle, still incensed with what had gone on in the schoolyard. Miss Perkins shushed them and tried to get things back to normal.

Finally the classroom got abnormally quiet. No one said another word but Hannah could tell that no one was concentrating on class work.

Miss Perkins went to the front and tapped her ruler on her desk to get their attention. She directed each student to get out their McGuffy readers and read the next chapter. Hannah tried to concentrate but she couldn't.

Finally Miss Perkins gave up and dismissed them early. Hannah knew for sure that Miss Perkins would spend the rest of the afternoon writing a letter of complaint to the school board about the actions of the bounty hunters and especially the sheriff. She had already written two other letters of complaint that year. One thing that Hannah always appreciated

148

about Miss Perkins what that she wasn't afraid to state her views.

As Hannah walked out to the road, some of the older girls crowded around her to talk to her. Their actions surprised her. Susan Green, who was the unofficial leader of all the older girls, put her hand on Hannah's shoulder.

"You did a brave thing today, Hannah. We wish we could have been that courageous." The girls around Susan nodded in agreement. Susan continued, "we'd like you to eat lunch with us tomorrow, if you want to. Lucinda's showing us all how to crochet. It's fun. We'll help you catch up."

When Susan saw the indecision on Hannah's face, she insisted.

"Please say yes. We're sorry for avoiding you before. Won't you please be a part of our group? We think you're a heroine." The rest of the group nodded once again. Susan continued. " Even Patrick and Paul say you had guts to stand up to that nasty bounty hunter like you did."

Patrick and Paul were the two tall boys who had flanked Miss Perkins at the gate hoping to protect her. Hannah smiled at the thought that everyone thought her a heroine.

Susan saw the smile and took it as an agreement. "Good tomorrow at noon then. If the weather is good, we'll meet out under the big oak. Don't worry about a crochet hook or yarn. We have enough extra supplies for you." Susan clapped her hands with relief. The rest of the girls giggled.

Cindy was still crying softly when Hannah went over to the hitching post to unhook her pony. She offered Cindy a ride home if she would finally stop her crying. The little girl made a half-hearted attempt at

150

smiling at the prospect of riding double with the new hero of the school. Soon the tears were forgotten with the thrill of riding home in style behind Hannah.

More Waiting

Tuesday morning Hannah woke up to the sound of heavy drumming rain on the roof. She crept out of bed and looked out the window. It seemed like the whole world was awash with water. Big puddles stood in the yard. Trees and flowers were bent down with the crush of the deluge. It was a good omen, she thought. The bounty hunters would have trouble tracking in this rain and the resulting mud and mire would slow the dogs and horses down.

But the bad news was, the cold rain and wind would not only slow down the hunters, it would slow down the slave girls. They wouldn't make good time in the drenching sheets of rain. And they wouldn't be able to stay warm or dry. And with this rain, the Ohio River would be running rough. Between the cold and the rain, the girls may not try to leave the island at all.

In her mind, Hannah had started calling the island, Ghost Island.

At breakfast, her mother made oatmeal for a change. "We need something today that is hot and will stick to our ribs." Hannah held Elizabeth and rocked her in the rocker, by the kitchen stove, while her mother stirred the boiling porridge.

"Make sure," Mrs. Haviland said to Hannah, "that you always support her head when you hold her."

Today was one of the first days that Hannah could remember in a long time when the whole family was going to eat breakfast together. It was too wet and windy for plowing. But the men had already been out to the barn to do their chores and feed and tend the animals.

They came in the back door with a stiff wind gusting around them. Water was pouring off their hats. Mr. Haviland and Aaron had on slickers to keep them dry but they didn't seem to help too much. They stamped their feet and took off the slickers and their hats and after banging them, hung them on pegs by the door to dry.

Before she left for school, her mother made Hannah don her wool cloak that had a hood that went over her bonnet to keep all her clothes dry. Besides the rain, a howling wind had sprung up, wailing and moaning around the eaves producing a ghostly sound.

Dark heavy clouds were scudding across the sky. Sunny spring had suddenly turned back into dreary winter. Hannah couldn't get the image out of her mind of Goodness and Mercy, barefoot and chilled, shivering with chills and a fever much like Elijah had.

Her father drove her to school in the buggy and she had to run pell mell up the steps and into the school room but the effort still didn't keep her dry. Her dress and bonnet stayed damp all day.

At school, indoor recess replaced the outdoor recess. The children divided into groups. The little students who needed to run off excess energy were playing tag down by the teacher's desk where Miss Perkins was grading papers.

The older boys played mumbly peg with their pocketknives in the cloakroom. The older girls gathered in the middle of the room to work on their crocheting, and as promised, they brought crocheting supplies for Hannah.

Several of the girls had sewing baskets that they had brought to school. Inside, the baskets were similar to the one her mother had at home. They held scissors, needles, and pins in pincushions, thimbles, a cloth tape measure, safety pins and dozens of spools of thread.

Susan showed Hannah how to take her yarn, tie a loop in the end to begin her chain. She learned how to put her crochet hook through the loop, grab a piece of yarn and pull it back through the loop to make another loop. She kept doing that over and over until she had a long chain of yellow yarn. Susan then showed her how to go back to the chain, beginning at the first loop, and repeat the process making a second chain that was hooked to the first. Each additional row made the original chain wider. Soon Hannah would have a small piece of crocheted work that she could use as a blanket for baby Elizabeth. Susan watched as Hannah's hands got

156

used to the stitch and they began to move faster and faster.

"Good job, Hannah. You catch on fast."

At lunchtime, the older girls asked Hannah to eat with them. She was starting to get used to spending time with them. She saw Jonathan across the room from her. He made a sign with one index finger touching his thumb. It meant that she was doing okay. It was nice to be a part of the group of six girls that told secrets, giggled over the boys' antics, crocheted and talked.

The girls were friendly now, asking Hannah to tell them all about her new sister and her beliefs as a Quaker. She told them that Quakers didn't believe in war and they didn't believe in slavery. During the crocheting time in the afternoon recess all the girls decided that it would be fun for all of them to crochet baby things for Elizabeth Rose.

"It can be our project," said Susan. "It's more fun if we all work toward a goal."

Soon the question came to Hannah. "Why do Quakers say thee and thou all the time?"

Hannah explained. "Quakers think that the word "you" should be reserved only for God. They use "thee" and "thou" for other human beings."

There was silence for a second, and then all the girls nodded. Stephanie said, "Makes sense in a way."

Hannah was thankful that they didn't bring up the black clothes. She didn't know what she would say if they brought up that touchy subject.

The rain hadn't let up by that evening. Hannah was depressed with the rain. She was depressed with the thought that maybe the slave girls hadn't even found the map or the food. The only cheering thought she had that night, as she was saying her prayers, was that the rain would wash away all evidence of the girls and that they would be safe from the trackers again.

That night she dreamed that Goodness and Mercy were snug and dry, sleeping inside a farmer's huge haystack. In the morning the rain had stopped but the ground and plants were soggy. But when Hannah saw the sun peeking through the scattering clouds, she was somehow cheered.

That afternoon, Hannah had lost her cheerful mood. She had heard other children discussing the runaway slaves and deciding that the odds were good that they would be captured and sent back to their Kentucky plantation.

When she met Jonathan at the hitching post, he was in a bad mood too. Evidently he had been having similar thoughts. He was wondering why they hadn't heard anything from Goodness and Mercy.

"It's been five days since we went over to the island. We should have seen some sign of them by now." It was one of the few times that Hannah had ever seen Jonathan frowning.

"It's really only been four days if thee doesn't count Saturday. And the bounty hunters were out searching on Monday. And then the rain storm..." Her words trailed off. She was only trying to make him feel better but it wasn't working. Jonathan's spirits were down. So were hers.

"They probably aren't even on that island!" Jonathan said fiercely. He was almost on the verge of tears. So was Hannah. They looked at each other. Jonathan shook his head.

"Where could they be?" he asked angrily. He then kicked a rock in the dirt in front of him. It went bouncing across the road. "I give up!" he shouted as he jumped on his horse and galloped off.

160

Hannah watched him disappear around a curve in the road. She was disappointed too. She was discouraged too. She was angry too. But she determined as she gritted her teeth, "I'm not going to give up...ever!"

Miss Perkins scolded Hannah on Thursday morning for daydreaming during math class and when she scolded her for the same thing in reading class she was assigned a recess detention. Hannah couldn't seem to stop herself from looking out the window and sighing. Jonathan also had lunch detention for not completing his spelling assignment. Miss Perkins was losing her patience with both of them. She sat down beside Hannah on the front porch as Hannah was clapping the erasers together to get the chalk dust out. Jonathan was out behind the building chopping wood for the wood box. Hannah could hear the thump, thump, thumping from the ax. In the meadow the children were playing tag. The crocheting club was meeting under the big oak.

Even though it was almost May, the wood box had been empty for a few weeks now from being used up in the winter. Miss Perkins clearly was mad when she had assigned Jonathan to fill it. It could have waited until fall, but Miss Perkins was so angry at their behavior that she was thinking up all the jobs she could to punish them for their lack of attention to studies.

She looked at Hannah closely while Hannah pounded the dust out of the erasers. "I want to know what's wrong with you and Jonathan today Hannah. Both of my two best students have been barely paying attention. You both have been sadly lacking in doing your homework or finishing your assignments. You both have been looking out the windows daydreaming and not paying attention. I won't have it! Do you hear me?"

Hannah had stopped clapping the erasers so that she could listen to Miss Perkins scold her. She hung her head and couldn't look Miss Perkins in the eye. She knew she was being a disappointment but she couldn't help it. She was worried about Goodness and Mercy and she couldn't concentrate on school. If the slave girls didn't find their map, she and Jonathan didn't have any other ideas.

"What's wrong? Tell me." Miss Perkins was almost hollering now. "I know something is wrong. What is it? Why are you two behaving so strangely?" It wasn't like Miss Perkins to scold and it was definitely not like her or Jonathan to be such poor scholars.

If she told Miss Perkins about the girls, she might be putting the girls in danger. Miss Perkins would just have to go on thinking that she and

Jonathan were being troublesome students. Hannah couldn't say anything; she just shook her head and started banging the erasers again.

Miss Perkins sighed as she stood up. She turned to go back up the steps to go back inside the school. But before she went in the doorway, she said, "You will be washing the windows when you are finished with those erasers." Hannah's silence had just made her madder.

That afternoon when Hannah got home so late, her mother was waiting for her in the kitchen, waiting for an explanation of why she had been kept after school.

"Did thee get in trouble today for being late this morning, Hannah?" "Not exactly," Hannah replied.

"What then?" Her mother had a frown on her face.

Hannah felt her lip quiver as she began telling her mother all the trouble she had gotten in at school. That she had been worried for the two slave girls and that when Miss Perkins asked her directly what was bothering her, she couldn't answer. She simply said that both she and Jonathan were worried and that they couldn't concentrate on their studies. Hannah was careful not to tell her mother that she had gone over to the island without permission. And she didn't tell about the map. That would be cause for another detention. This time a detention at home.

Her mother hugged her and told her to tend to her after school chores. At least her mother understood why she had been so distracted. It hurt her feelings that Miss Perkins was so angry with her. She had been such a good student in the past.

At dinner that night, her father didn't mention how late she had been with her chores. Neither did her brother tease her about it. Her mother must have told them that she was worried and that they shouldn't mention anything about it. Hannah went to bed depressed that nothing was working out that week, as it should.

She was so depressed that she couldn't even pray.

It was early Friday morning and Hannah was fighting with Old Biddy, trying to get eggs out of her nest. She finally gave up and decided to take what she had into the house. Biddy always got the other chickens upset and they would fly around the chicken coop making an awful fuss. She was just closing the chicken coop door when she heard a rustling in the bushes behind the pump. Her heart jumped. Not again! She looked and she could see that the bushes were shaking as if the wind was blowing.

She heard a noise. "Pssst." She walked over to the bushes and parted the bushes with one hand. Behind the leaves were two young black girls. She jumped with fright. She had been hoping all week and now here they were.

"Are thee Goodness and Mercy?" she asked. They both nodded. They had broken branches and leaves stuck in their hair. In fact their hair looked like it hadn't seen a brush in months. They were wearing shabby dresses and they had no shoes. Just like their father, they were full of bramble scratches.

"Come in the house, quickly." Hannah whispered, looking around for bounty hunters.

All three girls ran as fast as they could up on the porch and into the kitchen. Hannah's mother was at the stove and dropped the fork she was turning the bacon with when Hannah and the girls dashed in.

"My heavens. Are these Elijah's girls?" She asked, trying to get over her scare.

She looked at the girls and frowned at their dirty condition. "These girls need a bath and some clean clothes."

"And food." Hannah added as she noticed the girls eyeing the food on the table, all ready for breakfast. "They must be starving. They've been staying on Brect's Island, hiding from the patrols looking for them."

"How does thee know that, Hannah?" Mrs. Haviland asked as she added more bacon to the frying pan. She looked at her daughter raising her eyebrows. She motioned for the terrified girls to sit down and eat some bread and butter until the breakfast was finished. The girls gobbled the bread,

168

stuffing it in their mouths while Hannah explained to her mother how she and Jonathan had left a map on the island.

"Thee went to the island?" Her mother asked, anger in her voice. "Without asking?"

Hannah hung her head. She knew she was wrong to have gone without asking, but she was afraid everyone would have said no. She told her mother that.

"Certainly, I would have said no, Hannah. T'was a dangerous idea."

"But we were right. The girls were there. If thee had said no, they would still be lost."

Mrs. Haviland sighed. "I can't argue with that, Hannah. God has used thee to rescue these poor, hungry girls. But next time thee must let us know thy plans and we all can help."

"We need to get them washed up and into some clean clothes after breakfast." Mrs. Haviland added as she scooped more scrambled eggs onto the girls' plates.

After breakfast, Mr. Haviland and Aaron hauled water for the tub that was set up in the kitchen. By the time the two girls had bathed, Hannah had found some old black dresses that were too small for her to wear anymore.

Complete with two of Hannah's older bonnets, the twins looked like Quaker girls. All except for their black faces and bare feet. Unfortunately there were no shoes that would fit them

The whole family sat at the kitchen table after the girls had dressed. Mr. Haviland discussed with them what they needed to do next.

"We need to let the Olsen's know that we have more slaves to move north. It's very dangerous to keep them at the house for long. I was nervous just sitting down to eat breakfast. I kept waiting for the bounty hunters to show up."

"I think that after I go report to the Olsen's, we need to leave to take them north tonight. They can ride in the wagon under the hay just like Elijah. Is thee up for another trip, Aaron?"

"Yes, Papa. I'm ready."

Soon Aaron went to the barn to fix the wagon and load the hay. Mr. Haviland rode the big bay gelding to go let the Olsens know what was happening.

Mrs. Haviland went to fix a basket of food for the trip north while Hannah and the twins were left alone at the kitchen table to talk. Hannah asked them about the ghosts on the island.

"We did that, Miss Hannah," said the twin that Hannah knew was called Goodness. "We took some sheets and a lantern while we was traveling. When we got to the island, we tied the sheets high up in the trees and if someone was on the island at night, we'd light the lantern. They always thought what they was seeing was ghosts. They never stayed long to find out." The three girls giggled together.

Hannah's mother had just finished packing one basket with pies and bread and when that was filled, she then began wrapping some cold fried chicken into cloths and packing the bundle into the second basket.

She turned to the girls who were chatting together at the table. "We need to find a place for the girls to hide if the bounty hunters come looking

172

again. I have a feeling they won't be put off searching the house again."

"I have an idea, Mama." Said Hannah.

The words were barely out of her mouth when her father came running into the kitchen.

"Quick. Slave hunters on the road, five minutes behind me. Where can we hide the girls?"

"I know just the place, Papa. No one will find them there: The oak at Black Oak Meadow. No one would think to look there."

"Hurry!" Her father said. "Run."

Hurry and Hide

Hannah grabbed the hands of the two girls and ran with them down the lane toward the fields that Aaron and her father had just finished plowing. Behind them they could hear the hoof beats of the horses as they sped out of sight. The road was rutted and made the running hard.

Once Mercy fell and the two other girls stopped to help her to her feet. They could hear the men shouting to one another as they searched the barn and the yard. Hannah knew it was just a matter of minutes before they checked the fields. The girls had stopped holding hands and were just running as fast as they could. Hannah glanced back once and could see that the twin she called Mercy had fallen again. She ran back to help her up. A bramble scratched her across the cheek. She saw that Mercy had a deep cut in her right foot and that it was bleeding. She wrapped her arm around the younger girl's waist and dragged her along. Goodness was up ahead and stopped to wait. "Don't stop!" Hannah hissed at her. "Keep going!"

When they got to the end of the road, the partially plowed field spread out before them. Hannah motioned for them to follow her and from there they ran along the outside of the field, in the grass so they wouldn't leave footprints. All that was left was ducking under the bushes into the hollowed out tree. She could hear hoof beats getting closer. Could they make it? She pulled back the bushes and motioned for the girls to lean down to get inside the little room. No one looking from the field would even guess the tree would be a hiding place. Would they?

Just as she was ready to get into the tree herself, Hannah saw a horseman enter the field. Did he see her? Quickly she dove into the opening and pulled the bushes into place. Inside, they could hear the lone bounty hunter riding slowly back and forth across the field looking for clues.

The girls held their breath. Hannah put her finger to her lips as a signal to stay quiet. They sat down with their backs to the walls of the little black room and just waited in silence. No one moved. They heard the bounty hunter circling the fields again and again looking for them. Would he see their footprints in the dirt?

They finally heard the rider leave the field but they were afraid to move. It was better to just wait until her father came to say it was safe.

It was dark by the time Mr. Haviland came to get them. The twins were asleep and Hannah was just nodding off when she heard her father's soft whisper.

"Hannah?"

She woke the girls and they crawled out of their hidey-hole.

"Did the bounty hunters search the house, Papa?"

"They did Hannah. This time they came inside and looked everywhere. If thee hadn't thought of this place to hide, Goodness and Mercy would be on their way back to Kentucky by now. God has used thee twice to save these girls lives."

Hannah stood with her mother and baby sister in the yard watching the wagon loaded with hay turn into the road and head north. She was both sad and glad.

Glad that they were now safe and sad that she hadn't had much time to talk to Goodness and Mercy and get to know them.

She followed her mother back into the house, exhausted now that all the excitement of the day was over. She sat at the kitchen table with her mother and felt as if she would never be able to move again. She knew her face was scratched from the brambles and her hands and face were streaked with dirt and the black from the walls of the oak tree. She was dead tired. But it had been worth it. Goodness and Mercy were on their way to freedom and their father, Elijah.

Out of her pocket, her mother pulled a folded up piece of paper and handed it to Hannah. When she unfolded it, she realized that it was the map she had left on the island. Her mother must have hidden it in her pocket before the bounty hunters searched the house.

"This was a very good idea to bring the girls to our house for help, Hannah. I am proud of thee." Hannah smiled tiredly.

Mrs. Haviland continued, "I know that it has been hard for thee at school with thy dark clothes and all. I know thee likes colors so much and I can imagine that thee hates the black and gray that we Quakers have chosen to wear."

Hannah nodded, too tired to try to fool her mother any more about the dark clothes. How, she wondered, had her mother found out?

Her mother seemed to read her thoughts. "I've seen thee looking at the dresses and material at the store. I know how much thee loves to paint with color. Besides, when I turned eleven I started being ashamed of my clothes too. They seemed so drab and somber. I'm assuming that thee feels the same way. Am I right?"

Hannah nodded, feeling something like relief uncoiling inside her. Finally, at last she could tell her mother how she felt. Someone else would understand

180

how guilty she had been. It didn't seem right to hate her clothes. But she did. It felt better just to admit it.

She couldn't help explaining. "All the other girls have beautiful clothes and mine are so ugly. It's not fair." She was close to tears and she was definitely feeling sorry for herself.

"What if I told you there was a reason that we Quakers wore black and gray? And what if that reason has to do with slavery?"

Hannah sat up. She looked at her mother's serious face. She was no longer tired. Now her mother had her attention. "What? The black clothes have a meaning?"

"Not just a meaning, Hannah. A message. When Quakers decided to wear black and gray, it was to protest the fabric dyes that came out of the use of slaves. There would be no colorful clothing if it weren't for slave labor. When we wear black, we are saying to everyone and each other that we do not want to be a part of the slave trade. We each have to do what we can to make a difference. Everyone is made in the image of God. Our clothes make that message. Does thee understand?"

Hannah nodded, "I think so."

"Good," her mother said. " Black dresses and suits tell people around us that we are plain people. That we don't believe in slavery. That we don't believe that men are better than women; all are equal in the sight of God. When we wear black, we are telling others that we don't believe in war. We don't believe in killing. Black is a glorious message to all, Hannah. It is a beautiful color. When thee makes thy pictures, does thou not use dark colors to make shadows so that the light colors seem brighter?"

182

"Yes." Hannah nodded, starting to understand. Black was necessary too.

Hannah looked at her clothes and then at her mother. "I didn't know, Mama. I didn't know there was a reason for the black. I think that I will not be ashamed of my black clothes anymore."

"Good, Hannah. Now it is time to go to bed. Thee missed thy art day I'm sorry to say. But it was a good day anyway. Two more slaves are freed. Thee will have to think of an art project for next week."

"Yes," Hannah murmured. " But the one I want to do I can't do at school."

"Why is that, Hannah?"

"I can't do it at school, because Goodness and Mercy have to stay a secret, but when I saw them in Quaker clothes a new art project started forming in my mind. But at first, I didn't want to do it because it would just have to be black and white. But now I want to do it. I want to make sketches of Goodness and Mercy in Quaker clothes. I won't need colors," she laughed, smiling at her mother, " just charcoal and paper. But now I will love the black and white."